Tales of Christmas

Volume 1
8 Wonderful 'Feel Good' Stories

First Edition
MMXXII
Hot Armor Press

Diamond/DiAngelo Music and Books

Edited by R. H. Bauderer

ISBN: 9798361355396

This 'Book of Tales' is dedicated to:

First to my loving 'Mutter', who is 92 years young at the first printing of this book.

To my daughters, Brittany and Sabrina. And to my grandchildren, Angelo, Abella, & Ari.

To all of my friends, who I have known for so many years.

And of course, to all of you; that continue to read my tales and keep encouraging me to continue on this path of writing the words that stimulate your imagination.

Tales of Christmas could never be before you in published form if not for the hard work of R.H. Bauderer, (editing and formatting), and Rodney DiAngelo, (cover, back and spine design). Many, Many Thanks!

Lastly and most importantly, I give thanks to God for giving me the ability to write so many tales that are stored within my mind, and the ability to bring you along with me on some fantastic adventures within your own minds.

Tales of Christmas Volume 1, is also dedicated to all of you, who remember the Christmases of the past ... some so long ago, with memories that are very dear to many hearts.

It is the time of year where I have noticed, that even with the rushing about and stress of last minute shopping, people still reach out to help total strangers; and if nothing else, share a warm smile and a greeting of "Merry Christmas", on those cold December days.

Merry Christmas!

B. Diamond

In Loving Memory of a Special Lady
that I was blessed to have shared time with on
this winding road called life.

She is forever remembered for the time in
my youth, when the pathway of life was more
before me than behind.

Those crazy fun times in the 1980's will
be forever emblazoned in my mind and on my
heart.

Rest in Peace,
Gloria Maria Barbara Blouch,

... Until we meet again.

Table of Contents

Max and Charlie

Max was a very wealthy man who started his own courier service, and within ten years, only the 'big two' nationwide services were bigger than he was in his town. Although he started out as a simple and plain man, his wealth and drive to make more and more, money had consumed his once gentle soul. All he seemed to care about was the 'ole mighty dollar …even to the point where his wife and two young daughters felt left behind by his addiction.

It was Christmas Eve, and there was Max on the dock barking at his workers to keep up the pace on the last minute deliveries. As he went into his office his phone began to ring, and ring, and ring, but he was too busy looking up the profits of the busy day to answer. He leaned back in his chair, closed his eyes and began to calculate all the profits, which brought a big smile to his face. Deep in a train of thought with dollars signs filling his head, it was his secretary that brought him out of his "Green Dream", with a, "Mr. Robinson, Mr. Robinson … Max? Hello! Your wife is on line one."

Shooting her a "how dare you" look, he waved her off and answered the phone. His wife informed him that he had forgotten to pick up the gifts that were on lay-away, and the store was closing in one hour. Did he really have to put them on lay-away? Just to wait for the last minute price down? Brushing his wife off with, "I'll leave here in a second, and just remember, Christmas isn't real, but the money is!" Hanging up the phone he went back to the dock to make sure every little package had been sent out.

His wife knew too well that tone in Max's voice and decided to just drop the girls off at her parents' house, and pick up the presents herself. She got the girls ready and went on her way, while Max was once again consumed with money and profits. As Max was waiting for the last driver to get back, the others were busy preparing packages for Christmas. This year, it was either work the holiday or find another job. As the last man returned, Max bellowed, "Be here in the morning! 7 a.m. sharp! We should hopefully be done by noon. Anyone who calls in means you quit." Max followed that up by his now infamous, "Remember, Christmas isn't real, but the money is"!

Max looked at his watch and realized that the stores were closed. Telling his staff to "get out and be here in the morning", Max hurried into his office and opened his safe, which was filled was filled to the brim with money.

Grabbing a stack, he filled his pockets, and set four hundred dollar bills aside. He figured a hundred for each of the girls, and two hundred for his wife would be enough of a so called, "Christmas present". The rest of the money would end up in his safe at home.

Locking up, he made his way to the indoor parking garage. There he saw a man sitting against the wall with a box full of puppies. Thinking fast, he goes over and asks, 'How much for one?"

The ragged man with weather-torn eyes, smiles a toothless smile and replies, "Oh man, it's almost Christmas, whatever you can spare, be so nice and good."

Max with a big smile on his face, reaches into his pocket and pulls out the wad of money. Turning around so the man doesn't see, he fumbles through the hundreds, and finally finds a five dollar bill. "Here you go ... now which one..." Max see's one of the puppies already has a collar on, and knows he won't have to buy one.

Picking up the puppy, Max snips, "Ah this little bugger will do just fine" and walks off. Looking at the collar, he sees it has a name tag already on it, "Charlie".

Max now races home, and thinks, "Now I can give each of the girls a fifty dollar bill, and BOTH of them the puppy, and the other hundred will go into the safe at home." Looking down at the now sleeping puppy, he smiles and says, "See, Christmas isn't real, but the money is."

As he pulls up to the house he notices the lights are all off, "Good, not wasting electricity, more money in the pocket". Opening the garage, Max parks the car in and hurries into the house. Turning on the lights, he sees a note on the kitchen table that his wife had left, telling him that she was going to drop off the girls, and pick up the presents. Smiling again he pours himself a drink, and sits back in the recliner, dreaming of profits. Once again, he is interrupted ... this time by a call on his cell phone. Looking down at the caller I.D. he sees it's his in-laws.

Answering the phone, his wife's mother tells him, "Cassidy has not come by yet to drop off the girls, and I'm getting worried."

Brushing his mother in-law off, the profiteer assures her, "Cassidy probably just took the girls with her to pick up the presents, and after all, it's only Christmas Eve". Seeing head lights coming down the driveway, Max confirms his theory to his mother in -law and hangs up the phone. The car stops outside, and within a few minutes the doorbell rings. Thinking her arms are full, and the girls are not helping, Max hastily marches to the door and swings it open. Expecting to see his wife and girls, it's just a young State Trooper, with bright red hair and freckles. Looking at him a bit confused, "And so, how can I help you, Opie Taylor."

The young Trooper politely asks if he can come in.
Max waves him in and asks him, "So, what's this all about?"

Looking at Max, the Trooper begins to speak.
"Are you Max Robinson?"

Looking annoyed at the young officer, Max replies
"Yes, yes. What the heck is this all about? Did someone ship
a package through my company with something illegal in it?
I am protected from this sort of thing, should I call my lawyer?"

With a serious look, the State Trooper interrupts,
"No! Please! Mr. Robinson, sit down, I have some very bad
news for you."

Max backs off a bit stunned and sits back in his recliner
and grabs his drink. Inside of him his stomach is telling him
something isn't right.

Looking at Max with compassion the Trooper speaks,
"Mr. Robinson, it's with my deepest regrets I must inform you,
your wife and children, were fatalities in a hit and run accident,
less than a mile from here. We are frantically looking for the
suspects as they fled the vehicle."

Max's face begins to turn from an angry annoyed red, to a
pale white. Just as the horrifying news begins to sink in, a
yelping puppy's bark breaks the silence; Charlie was awake,
and all alone in the car, in the cold dark garage.

And so…this Christmas Tale of Max and Charlie
begins now….

A snowflake gently lands and melts on weather beaten hands,
He hurriedly gathers his trinkets, his dog, and his aluminum cans;
It was Christmas Eve and there's a big storm coming,
Having been warned sent the whole town running.

The man knew there would be no bed for them tonight,
Where the Cross always glows its heavenly light;
Having saved all his coin, and dollars, for a day like today.
He had two things left to sell, and then he too could pay

For a place nice and warm for he and his friend,
It's been eleven long years since life came to an end;
All that Max had was Charlie, and Charlie just Max,
They left that night together and they never looked back.

As the flakes became bigger, they had just enough time,
To sell some new shoes and a coat they did find;
The new shoes were too small and the coat just as well,
From a delivery truck, they bounced out and fell.

A pawn shop would give him for these and his ring,
Some money to live for a few days like kings;
With a smile on his face, and tail wagging behind,
They hurried to sell what they today did find.

The snow getting harder and daylight becomes dim,
The pawn shop was in view, they were both almost in;
When a cry from an alley interrupted the still night,
The sound of a child's anguish of hunger and fright.

As Max turned the corner, with Charlie in tow,
They saw a young boy sitting cold down below;
He had no coat, and his shoes full of holes,
His eyes full of tears as he looked at these souls.

Max asked him his name, but the boy did not speak,
Was he too frightened? Too cold or too weak?
   Max looked at Charlie, there was only one thing to do,
Give the boy the things that were meant for these two.

   Max left Charlie with the boy, and off he did run,
Across to the pawn shop, just under the gun;
   With no coat or shoes and only his wedding ring,
Max knew in his soul, it was the right thing.

   With money in hand, Max came back to the two,
The warm coat now on him, then the left and right shoe;
   The boys tears were gone, and a smile in its place,
Max had never seen such and innocent face.

   He knew of a place where the boy could alone stay,
A price that he and Charlie, were willing to pay;
   The three set out through the storm and the night,
To the warmth of a place with a bright neon light.

   With the boys room paid, and a meal on the go,
Max and Charlie headed back outside into the snow;
   One last look back, the boy no longer meek,
A wave good-bye, for he never did speak.

   Max only had Charlie, but was now content,
The money was needed, all gone but well spent;
   Max picked up Charlie and hurried across the street,
Not seeing the ice, he soon slipped off his feet.

   Charlie bounced once and on a snowdrift did sit,
Along came a car, not seen and was hit;
   Max rushed and scrambled to his best friends side,
As the snow turned to red, he sat down and cried.

Max picked up Charlie and rushed through the street,
As if the wings of Mercury were upon both his feet;
The animal hospital was open every night, every day,
Max did not know how, but someday would pay.

Yelling "It's almost Christmas could you help me with this?"
The man shook his head, "Christmas isn't real, but the money is."
So with Charlie in his arms Max went back outside,
Found him some shelter and a dark place to hide.

Holding Charlie so close, his little heartbeat real slow,
Max's eyes opened up, and tears began to flow;
Max cried out "Why me? Why me, once again?"
"Eleven years later, had I not paid for my sins?"

Max looked down at Charlie, blood filling his side,
The side wound too great, poor Charlie had died;
As Max held close his friend oh so dear,
Out of the darkness a strange light did appear.

And in the light a small shadow arose,
He could soon see a face and a small little nose;
It was the boy he helped earlier, he began to sing,
Then Max saw not one, but two silver wings.

As the boy finished singing, his face was aglow,
"Max I am Christmas, the Christmas you now feel and show";
"I am the Christmas Angel who so long ago"
"Announced a birth so all mankind would know".

"For the kindness you have given this blessed night,
All sorrows be removed, and all wrongs made right";
As The Boy raised his hands, Max felt love so deep,
His head became dizzy, and he soon fell asleep ...

"Mr. Robinson, Mr. Robinson, Max! Hello! Your wife is on line one."

As Max opened his eyes he was back in his office. Looking at his secretary, 'Um, what? This can't be?"

She looks at him, "Ok, I don't know what's wrong with you, but your wife, line one."

As she leaves, Max timidly picks up the line, "Hello?" And as the voice on the other end reminds him of the layaway, Max's eyes fill with tears and he tries his best to control himself. Telling her to stay put, he is leaving right now, and will be home to get her and the girls right away and they can all go together, straight to the store. With a frog in his throat the words come out, "I love you all so much."

Cassidy is stunned and pleased by his over caring tone, and thinks, "Maybe Christmas for Max does have a miracle or two left in it".

Max then rushes to the safe, fills his pockets and a suitcase full of cash, and rushes downstairs.

"Stop! Stop working! We are done for the day, and for those people who ordered too late, well they'll get their stuff, on the 26th, oh what the heck, the 27th! Here take this suitcase and divide it up between yourselves, Merry Christmas!"

Max leaves the suitcase on the table and rushes down to the parking garage. He is running so fast that he barely catches a glimpse of a man selling puppies.

He runs over, looks down and sees one with a collar. "How much for them all?!"

The man looks at Max, "I'm sorry sir, they are all sold, all but the one with the collar. But I don't know if you want that one, he's got a birth defect."

Max looks at the man, "What defect?" The man picks up the puppy and flips him over, "See, right here on his side, he got some big scar looking thing. He must have been born with it."

As Max picks up Charlie, their eyes both know what has just happened. "I'll take him, he's perfect! And here," Max reaches in his pocket and hands the man his wad of money.

"MERRY CHRISTMAS!" Holding Charlie real close he walks a few steps and turns to the man, "So who bought the rest of the puppies?"

The man looks at Max, "some boy, with new shoes and a new coat, and the most innocent eyes I ever seen, he said he had to fly …but will be back."

Spiritus Nativitatis

(The Spirit of Christmas)

Part 1 of 'The Trilogy'

The clouds were hanging low on this particular morning in the big city; the 24th of December. There was a chill in the air and a good chance it could be the first white Christmas in years. Among the city's millions of inhabitants, three people would share something in common … something that would impact the rest of their lives.

Susan had come into the city with a couple of friends, not just to enjoy the scenery and Christmas decor, but to see if there's anything that she does not have yet. Susan, Vickie and Lynn are what you call, super privileged. They had always been surrounded by the best things money had to offer. All three had been in the best boarding schools and are now ready to graduate from their prestigious colleges, though none plan on doing anything with their degrees, because of multimillion dollar trust funds. To them it's just a high society standard. There is only a slight exception to the three; Susan was not always this way.

Susan's fortune came through her mother's second marriage with one of the richest lawyers in the country. Susan does remember her real dad from time to time, although she tries not to, because of painful memories.

She remembers how rare it was to see him as a little girl growing up. She still dreams of his smile and his laughter from time to time. She still has memories of going to church with him, and how the inside of the huge cathedral had always left a smile on her face. It was like a whole different world for her young innocent eyes to behold. Susan remembers a silver locket with, "I Love You', Dad" on the back and the Virgin Mary on the front. But all of this is lost … first the faith as her step father was an Atheist, with money being his God. Then she lost her locket while on a vacation on some Caribbean island. Then came that terrible day, September 11th, 2001, when her father, a firefighter was called into action … for the last time. Even with the finest places and things money can buy, Susan still carries an emptiness inside that all her luxury can never fill.

~~~~~~

Mike was busy looking through the finest jewelry shops for that 'one of a kind' special gift for a lady. This gift needed to be as exquisite as the person for whom it is intended. Mike was another one who never had a shortage of money. Just twenty years after starting out on his own, as a young man, he now owns one of the biggest brokerage firms in the country, and he's still only in his forties. Lady luck has always been close by his side. His gift could be nothing less than what would be expected to be presented to a woman whose beauty rivals that of Helen of Troy. But sometimes beauty can blind you, as his gift for "Helen" would be many times greater than what he would spend on his wife, Paula, and their three children.

Mike had always played the odds ever since he was a young boy. His parents were mysteriously killed while in Africa and Mike grew up on an estate with his grandfather, a hard drinking, gambling, betting man, who taught Mike how to survive. Love was never taught, shown, or spoken of. Instead he was taught, how to take a suckers money. This was an everyday lesson that Mike soon perfected. Then came the day that his gambling, hustling, grandfather died, after a Herculean whiskey binge. Mike was just seventeen. Since then he had learned that life is filled with millions of dollars, just waiting for the taking.

With "Helen's" advances, the time was right to bet all he had invested into his marriage, on the beauty of a sure thing.

~~~~~~

Unlike Susan and Mike, whose destinies will soon collide with his, Jamal struggles from paycheck to paycheck. Driving for a taxi service, Jamal has worked hard to get what little things he has. Having grown up in the inner city, Jamal's life has been anything but privileged. If he had any luck at all, it would be bad.

Jamal remembers little about his father, only that he played his old guitar on weekends over on the street corner to earn a few extra dollars. Gang violence had claimed its first family victim, when his father was hit by a stray bullet while playing the blues. His mother did what she could to work two jobs to provide for Jamal and his two older brothers, but to no avail. All the love she had inside could not keep her two oldest sons away from a life of tragedy.

Jamal's oldest brother was killed in a gang shootout over drugs. In retaliation, his other brother shot four rival gang members to death, and was sentenced to life in prison. To top this off, at sixteen, Jamal's mother was diagnosed with breast cancer, and died a year later. All the bad in his life, would have been too much for many, but Jamal was a fighter, and he refused to throw in the towel.

Before his mother died, she set Jamal up with the pastor of the local church, a place where he could live and work, until he was old enough to make it on his own, with no gangster guiding his reins. She also gave Jamal his father's old guitar, and in just a very short time; his fingers would be sliding over the strings like butter over a hot skillet. Jamal not only taught himself to read music, but to memorize and play anything he had heard. It was then that he fell in love with 'classical music'. What was once played on piano, organ, violin, or cello, Jamal could play note for note on a simple old blues guitar.

After graduating high school, Jamal enrolled at a community college for a degree in music. His music professor soon saw something special in the young lad and arranged an audition for a chance to study at the highly acclaimed Universidad de Alicante in Madrid Spain. Only fifteen people in the world are given this chance per year. Jamal had heard nothing back from the prestigious school, and with a new semester soon beginning he figured he knew the answer. On top of all of this, Jamal's guitar, his most cherished possession, was stolen from his apartment. The last thing his father ever touched gone. And now his car needed major work and his rent would increase at the beginning of January. Money was short and luck, again, all bad.

There was one possibility for the young struggling man … an old acquaintance of his brothers, had offered Jamal two thousand dollars for a one time 'drop off' in the inner-city. He would need to meet up with him by noon. Times were tough, what to do? One of the last things Jamal had promised his mother was that he would stay clear of any and all those that had destroyed his father and brothers. She knew, one small step, and like a fly on the outskirts of a spiders web, once in, you can't get out.

Snowflakes began to float out of the gray skies, as millions rustled about the maze of towering skyscrapers... For a twenty two year old blond, a middle aged white man with the 'itch' and a young, no luck, taxi driving black man, destiny was quickly heading their way.

As Susan walked out of the high end coffee shop, she did not see the figure approaching her and ran right into it. With a bump that almost knocked her down,

"What the Hell! Why can't you watch where you're going?" Susan blurts out as she looks down at the coffee that was now all over her designer jacket. "My God Mr. Homeless Man, this jacket is worth more than you can panhandle in a year".

Vicky and Lynn try to use their napkins to help wipe the dripping coffee off Susan's designer attire.

Vicky gets a snotty look on her face, "Susan, you should have this man arrested; I think he tried to grab you improperly."

All three are now fussing about, when Susan notices the man with long white hair bent over, feeling his way along the sidewalk until his hands find his sunglasses and he puts them back on. Slowly getting back up on his feet, Susan's eyes focus on the cane. Vicky and Lynn keep insulting the stranger, while still soaking up the coffee spillage.
Susan looks at this man before her … tall, long white hair, with a big green bag hanging off his shoulder. A strange emotion suddenly hits her. Something she has never felt before … pity.

Standing before her the man just smiles, "I'm sorry young lady".

Vicky and Lynn continue to insult the man and out of nowhere Susan yells, "Won't you two just shut up!"

Vicky and Lynn look at Susan, then at each other and Vicky's eyes become filled with rage, "What did you just say to Lynn and me? Listen here; if your mommy wasn't good looking and good at pleasing her 'sugar daddy', you would have grown up with nothing, because we know it all. Yes Susan we've always known that your real daddy was a poor loser fireman. He probably ran into those towers so he wouldn't have to deal with his bratty kid and slutty ex-wife anymore."

Susan looks at the old blind man for a second, "Excuse me for a second Sir".

Looking first at Lynn, then at Vicky, she smiles, then punches Vicky square in the nose.
Vicky startled and shocked at what just happened, grabs Lynn's hand the two begin to scamper away as blood begins to trickle down Vicky's face as onlookers begin to chuckle.
Vicky looks back, tears in her eyes, "I'm gonna sue you Susan! You can count on that! Come on Lynn, she is dead to us, dead!"

As the two disappear into the crowd, the blind man clears his throat, "You know she's going to sue you".

Susan smiles, "Yeah, but my step dad's a lawyer, THE lawyer. And you know what? Frankly, I don't even care. Are you okay? I'm soooo sorry. Is there anything I can do for you? Please. I don't know why, but I feel something inside …something that I haven't felt since, well, since a long time ago."

Standing up straight, his white hair catching snowflakes in the wind, "Well, I have two little favors, first, it's been a while since I had a good cup of coffee, and if it tastes as good as it smells, you can even pour a little on me if you like. Second, right down the street by the Y, there's a little place where they let people play music. The area is under an awning, and it has a heater. Get me a coffee, bring it over and come listen to just one of my songs."

Susan laughs, "You got it, after all, I don't have friends anymore, and well, I really never did. Sure, see you in about ten. Did you want me to guide you there?"

Brandishing a big smile, "Young lady, I'll meet you there, after all, guidance is what has brought me to you"

Susan laughs again as the man turns and walks on, cane melodically tapping in front.

Mike is now scrambling about. His chauffer is franticly driving from one high-end jeweler to an even higher end jeweler. Mike is getting frustrated, for he is meeting "Helen" in an hour and has no present. Knowing he can only be with her for a short time, before he needs to get back to his penthouse and wife and kids, he starts yelling at his driver,

"Damnit Clyde! Just run the damn red lights, I'll pay the stupid ticket!"
As the limo begins frantically changing lanes and running red lights, Mike taps Clyde on the shoulder, "Next street, Joeltec Custom Jewelry, turn right, fast!"

Looking back and acknowledging Mike, the limo begins its right turn through the light, not seeing the man with the cane in the crossing. Slamming on his brakes with a jolt to Mike in the back, there is still an impact as the cane and sunglasses go flying before the limo comes to a stop.

"Ah crap!" Mike yells as he jumps out to see the man with long white hair lying in the street.
Mike looks down, "Hey, you okay? Please let me help you up"
The blind man feels for his bag, it's still intact.
Then the blind eyes look toward Mike, "Son a be-gun, haven't had a jolt like that since the running of the bulls in 85."
Clyde is now beside the man helping him to his feet. Mike begins to feel nervous about this accident, so the negotiating business side kicks in,

"Hey Old Timer, you look ok, don't seem to have broken anything, how about we just settle this with a few Ben Franklins and call it even?" Looking at his Rolex, Mike knows his shopping time is almost up.

Putting his glasses back on as Clyde hands him his cane, the blind man smiles back at Mike, "No, you see, I have no use for those, I can't tell the difference between them and a George Washington. But, you know, I sure could use a big sub sandwich, and I smell a steak and cheese from somewhere close. Oh, and one more thing, you need to listen to me play and sing a song on the corner, the cafe by the Y as soon as you get my sandwich."

Mike looks at his watch, then at Clyde. Thinking, "I could just agree and leave, this man is blind, and he'll never know us". Glancing again at his watch, Mike is just about to make a decision when a young black man approaches. "Hey ole guy, you okay? I was parked across the street for a second, waiting for a package when I saw what happened."

The white hair again blowing in the wind, the old man turns and faces the voice, "Oh I'm fine, this man is going to get me a sandwich and listen to me play a song, then we'll be even Steven."

Mike looks at the young man, who suddenly recognizes him, "Hey I know you, I've seen you on all those financial pages, you're ..."

Mike cuts him off, "A man who needs to grab a steak and cheese"

The sunglasses turn towards Mike, "... and potato chips, plain Lays, no one can eat just one".

Nervously glancing at his watch, Mike reaches into his pocket and grabs his wallet. Handing Clyde his Platinum Black card, "Go to Joeltec's; tell the owner Brian, I want the Amazon Red Starr Ruby Pendent. Then meet me at the Y."

Looking back at the blind man, "Okay, I'll meet you over at the café by the Y as soon as I get your food, you play your song, and then as you said, we'll be even Steven"

Again a big smile appears on a blind man's face, "Yup, you'll never owe anything again."

Mike hurries off to place the order as the young black man looks at his watch. Glancing across the street he sees a man with a package approaching his parked car.

Just as he's about to leave the old blind man speaks up, "You mind giving me a hand crossing this street? I mean what could be next, Santa and his reindeer running me over?"

Jamal sees the guy now waiting by his car, one package, two thousand dollars. Glancing at the blind guy, white hair gently blowing in the wind with a big smile before him, Jamal thinks, "Damn, if it wasn't for this guy, I'd be on my way, just one time, and debt free."

Noticing the man standing by his car is getting nervous by his absence, "All right old guy, you have no idea what you're costing me, hang on, grab a hold of my arm and be prepared to walk fast".

As the light changes Jamal yells, "Let's Go!", and with the old man in tow he hurries them both across the street.

The stranger a bit out of breath, "Thanks young man, say, you ever heard an old man play guitar?"

Jamal was just about to dash off when the old guys words freeze him in his tracks. "What? You play guitar?"

Smiling at Jamal and his baffled look upon his face, "Yeah I do, and I will in a few minutes, right down this very street outside at the café by the Y, come on join me. But do me one favor first." Taking the bag across his shoulder off, "Make sure she's still ok, I've got her wrapped up with some of that bubble wrap I found, but I want to make sure."

Jamal grabs the bag and pulls out the object encased in bubble wrap. Unwrapping it carefully Jamal's eyes widen as he sees the guitar. Having done a research paper on classic guitars and builders, Jamal was almost certain this guitar is an original 1930's classical built by the legendary guitar maker Jose Ramirez himself. It even had custom engraving and wording on it. Looking at the grinning blind man before him, "yes, she's fine. Do you know what this is? I mean you better be careful who sees this, it's worth, well … a bunch." Tapping Jamal on the leg, "Come on Einstein, I got a few songs to play before the weather gets too bad" No sooner had the blind guitarist said his words, that the gray skies turned darker and big flakes begin to fill the tall towering skyline.

Leading the white-haired snow covered man down the street, Jamal glances back toward his car and what now is an angry man with a package. Thinking to himself, "Alright momma, you win".

Getting under cover and under some heaters, Jamal grabs a chair for the old man. "Here ya go, dry and warm, have a seat. I can make sure your guitar is in tune if you want?"

With his patient smile, "of course young man, you know my hearing isn't what it used to be, and with all this traffic and street noise in the background, I'm much obliged"

Tuning it up Jamal is still in awe of what he is holding and now strumming. Handing the guitar over to the old weathered hands, 'Here you go, it's all ready for you."

Taking the guitar the old man leans back in his chair against the wall. Strumming it a bit he quietly says to himself, "not yet, not just yet".

The wind blows a bit and the smell of coffee and steak and cheese sandwich fills his nostrils. "Now".

As he begins to play, the dark skies and falling snow along with the Christmas lights and decorations, enhance this Spiritual moment. As he continues to play, Susan's eyes widen, Mikes inpatient urge subsides and Jamal's despair for money fades away. As soon as the old voice begins to sing along with the magical fingers on his old guitar, passersby are also attracted to the sounds of Christmas that are enchanting their ears on this street corner.

Mike could have left as Clyde parked the limo.

Susan could have been with Vicky and Lynn at some festive high class dinner party.

Jamal could have dropped off a package and fixed his car and had rent.

All three are now transfixed on the white-haired blind man and his heavenly songs.

Susan still with a coffee in hand, Mike with a brown paper bag, sandwich and Lays potato chips inside and Jamal watching a guitar performance of a lifetime.
Clyde walks up and hands Mike back his card along with the ruby pendant.

After thirty minutes and a massive amount of onlookers, just as it started, the music stops, to a thunderous applause from the masses. With a smile forming below the dark shaded glasses, the man stands, and politely bows. Knowing that he has touched so many, including the three special spectators, he calmly speaks once the appreciation dies down.

"Thank you, Merry Christmas, God Bless, and pass it on."
Sitting back down the crowd begins to disperse.
Smelling the now not so hot coffee and not so warm sandwich, "Well, I can use a bite and a drink."

The three just stand in silence and watch as the old white-haired stranger devours the meal and drink. Rubbing his stomach, "Wow now that was a treat. Well since I'm here close to the Y, think I'll go in and take a quick shower"

Jamal steps forward, "I can take you to the entrance if you like?"

Again smiling, "Jamal, young man, I'm blind, and old, do you want them thinking I'm handicapped too?
Now, since I think you, Susan and Mike are still around, you can do me a favor, hold onto my prized possessions till I get out, you know some would even steal from a blind man in there."

"Anyway, Susan … here, let me get this out of my bag, I know it looks like an old little wooden box; but what's inside is kinda cool. Take a peak while I'm inside if you want to.
And Mike, here, I've had this a while, even the old envelope is showing its age, just a little old reading material to pass the time. And as for you Jamal, just hang on to my old six string lady. You can make her sing a bit if you like. Now, I'll grab my bag and I think the entrance is about thirty paces down and to the right, see you all in about thirty minutes or so."
Standing up the figure begins to walk a few steps as the snow flies around his head, "Hey Mike, show some hospitality and let them others sit in your big fancy car and wait, you can catch a cold out here you know! "

Susan and Jamal join Mike and Clyde in the warm roomy limo as the white-haired blind man taps his way to the entrance.

With Clyde up front, the three back seat drivers sit for a second just looking at each other not knowing what to say. It's Jamal that breaks the silence, "You know this guitar I am holding was once made by one of the finest guitar makers ever. It's got to be at least 75 years old".

Susan and Mike acknowledge Jamal, and just sit there smiling. Finally Clyde speaks up, "Hey I was just thinking, Jamal, you know any Christmas songs?"

With a big smile, "You bet I do, here's a Classic"

Jamal begins to play, as Susan's and Mike's eyes indicate that this is an extremely good young guitaris

Jamal plays about five heavenly tunes to the delight of all. As soon as he hits his last note, all the others give him a "Bravo" and much praise. Then silence again fills the big car.

Clyde once again breaks the silence, turning around and looking at Mike, "Mr. Garrison, something puzzles me, how did that man know our names? After all he was blind and wouldn't have recognized you." Mike gets a puzzled look on his face.

Jamal has the same look, "Yeah, he called me by my name too, I never told him."

Susan chimes in, "well he must have heard my former friends say my name, but yeah in both your cases, that is strange."

Clyde speaks up again, "But how did he know my name?"

After a few minutes they all start talking and trying to figure things out. Jamal holding the guitar, Mike the envelope and Susan a little wooden box.

Clyde notices the time, "Um, don't mean to interrupt, but it's been almost an hour, think we should check on our Y guest?" All three in the back lay down their things and get out as Clyde rushes around and opens the door. Quickly making their way to the front door, it was almost like an old comedy movie as they all try to enter through at the same time.

Once inside Jamal looks at the wide eyed man behind the front counter, "Has the blind man finished cleaning up yet?"

With a mystifying look the man replies, "What blind man?" Susan rushes to the counter, "The old white-haired man with sunglasses and a cane!"

The man just shakes his head, "look honey, till you four tried to take out the doorway, no one soul has come in or out in 2 hours. In fifteen minutes I am out of here, it's Christmas Eve you know."

Mike clearly concerned, speaks up, "Do you mind if we take a look around? We all saw him walk down here; maybe you looked away or left for a few seconds?"

Now the man flashes a stern look, "Okay, that's it, I don't know how much spiked eggnog or whatever you all have had, leave or I'll call the cops." The man points towards the door and all hesitantly leave and walk back to the limo and get inside.

Susan picks up the little wooden box she left on the seat, as Mike picks up the envelope. Lifting up the top Susan is completely startled at what she sees inside. Mike too opens the envelope, pulls out an item and has an astonished look on his face. All the while Jamal is holding the 1930's Ramirez guitar in his hands.

Susan lets out a scream and tears begin to roll. "It can't be! How? Oh My God!" Lifting the item out of the box, she turns it over, "It is" Looking at the others she slips the chain over her neck.

"My father bought this for me many years ago when I was just a little girl. He was one of the Firemen killed in the Trade Center attacks. I lost this a few years later on a beach in the Caribbean."

Mike looks at Susan and Jamal, and then shows what was in the envelope with disbelief.

"Wow, this here is a journal, diary, some kind of record of my parent's trip to Africa. The picture on the cover are my parents holding a small toddler, me."
Stopping for a few seconds and reading, Mikes eyes tear up, "Seems they were in Africa to help disabled children. It says they were missing me, and couldn't wait to come home to their estate." Thumbing through the books pictures of disadvantaged kids and reading a few of the captions, Mike pulls out a newspaper clipping in the back and reads it, "Society Elites, Michael and Judy Garrison Killed in African Plane Crash, Son Orphaned." Laying it down, "Now where did that blind man get this and know to give it to me?"

Susan stares out into the snow, "and how did he know to give this back to me?"

Jamal strums the guitar gently, "Yeah, kind of freaky, we all got something we didn't expect, and the dude disappears, on Christmas Eve."

Clyde starts the car, "Mr. Garrison, your family's waiting, shall we drop our guests off where they wish and be on our way?"
Mike nods his head and the long silver Christmas Eve six door sled, rolls on.

One year later … on Christmas Eve … three lives have changed due to a long white-haired blind stranger.

Susan never went back to her friends. As a matter fact she went back to church where she met a young Italian American fireman, he will propose to her that night. She uses her trust fund to donate money and time to orphaned and needy children in the great city. This year she alone has supplied over three thousand gifts to those who have little. The Locket with, "I love you … Dad", is forever placed around her neck.

For Mike that journal held the truth of how his drunken grandfather squandered and bet away his parent's fortune. It also conveyed how much his parents loved him; something he had never felt before. After dropping off his guests that Christmas Eve a year earlier, Mike spotted a Red Kettle bell ringer. He had Clyde stop, Mike got out and dropped the Amazon Red Starr in the pot. He and his wife Paula then made plans to move away with their three children. He sold his brokerage, moved west to Colorado, and opened a special ranch for kids with disabilities. The special kids and their parents would always be non-paying guests. And Clyde … he exchanged his suit and tie for jeans and a cowboy hat and is now the special ranch's buckboard driver.

Jamal had made the right choice that day a year before; another man delivered the package and he was robbed and shot dead. Jamal walked up the steps to his apartment that last Christmas Eve night, finding the neighbor lady standing there with an envelope. She had been gone, and this letter had been accidently placed in her mailbox. Jamal had been accepted with a full scholarship to the Universidad de Alicante.

Having impressed his teachers and others, Jamal was invited this Christmas Eve to play for a very special 200th anniversary of a Christmas song written by Joseph Mohr at a church in Oberndorf bei Salzburg in Austria. Carefully taking out his Classic 1930's Ramirez with the special etchings and engraved "Spiritus Christi" on it; Jamal sits in the front pew.

A young Priest walks by and sees the beautiful guitar. "Wow what a beauty ... and Christmas Spirit".

Jamal smiles, "Thank you; yeah she's a beauty and Christmas Spirit to you."

The Priest grins, "No I mean that engraving on your guitar, it reads, Spiritus Christi, that's Latin for Christmas Spirit."

Jamal gets that strange feeling again, just like he had a year earlier. The Priest sits down and reaches out his hand, "I am Father Stefan, music director for tonight's special event." Jamal grabs his hand, "Jamal Connor, from America and the prestigious Alicante Music School in Madrid."

Father Stefan gets a surprised look, "Wait, you are Jamal Connor, Yes?"

Jamal nods, "yeah the one and only".
The priest gets up and runs to the back.

Jamal begins to think, "What the heck is that all about? I've been invited to play; hope there's no mess up".

Suddenly Father Stefan taps him on the shoulder.

"Here, a man left this for you last Christmas Eve; he said you'd be here sometime to pick it up."

Jamal's eyes get big as he sees a familiar greenish bag. Untying it carefully, Jamal looks inside, and then his eyes begin to show his emotions. "What did this man look like, last year?"

Father Stefan thinks, "Well, I remember he was tall, long white hair, sunglasses, a cane. At first I thought he was a homeless blind man, until he touched me. Don't ask me how I knew, but I knew he was …."

Jamal wipes his eyes, "He was what?"

The Priest looks towards the ceiling, "Not like any on this Earth".

The church is packed for the 200th anniversary rendition of Josephus Franciscus Mohr's classic Christmas song. Jamal is poised, guitar in hand, ready as he is given the cue to play. The Classic 1930's Special Ramirez shines immensely as it sits on the guitar stand, behind the guitarist. Jamal began to play on the old beat up faded guitar that had once played the blues so long ago. As the microphones pick up every plucked string note, the choir joins in. After a blessed year, this young man from the inner city knows that Christmas and the Christmas Spirit are truly real.

Especially today, in this place, right now;

On this "Silent Night".

The Gift

Jürgen was on the hunt. His prey would take him into many hidden places and dark shadows, and he was determined to make the kill when it came time. It is the winter month of December, the 23rd day of the year 1944. Germany is on the defensive, as the allies begin to squeeze their once conquered territories into smaller and smaller spaces, driving them back into their original lands. Jürgen is proud to have graduated at the age of 17, and become a member of the supreme German military faction known for their brutal toughness. He was SS. With men in short supply, and invaders approaching from all directions, the Nazi High Command needed new recruits to fill the spots of those that have been killed or captured.

Jürgen's ordeal began two years earlier when he lost his whole family in Nuremberg. He was at the church that night playing music and singing, in preparation for the next nights Christmas Eve performance. It was in the middle of rehearsal that the allied planes devastated the city. That night he found his home completely leveled, and his family consumed in the flames. That Christmas Eve he met a Nazi party official, who told him, "The pilots and bombardiers were the Jews that got away, and now fly for the Allies." Jürgen left the church that day and headed down the path of….Evil.

Jürgen was not looking for a deer, boar, or other wild game … he was on the hunt for Jews. It seems there had been a break out and his orders where to find and 'eliminate' any and all escaped Jews, including men, women, and children. This being his first assignment, he was anticipating the killing of his first Jew, for what they did to him and his family. Revenge and hate had been drilled into the boy's heart since that fateful night, two years earlier.

He and his "hunting" patrol were just about to settle down when allied troops spotted them and a battle broke out. Jürgen was the only one who survived the night, and had made a dash into the woods, where he hid all day, until the night once again settled in. It was the 24th of December, and this seventeen year old 'Storm Trooper' was somewhere in southeastern Germany, alone. He had lost his compass during the skirmish, and had dropped his rifle; all he had left was his Luger and 6 bullets. He also managed to have just a little food, including a chocolate bar he was saving.

As he creeps quietly along the deep brush in the woods, he now sees a dim light in the distance. As he approaches cautiously, he notices a little house next to a bombed out little church.

Taking his time getting there, he quietly peaks around the corners and peers through the cracks in the wooden window blinds; to see a shadow inside moving about. He nervously approaches the front door, pulls his pistol, and kicks it in!

Once inside he immediately slams the door shut behind him. Shakily pointing his Luger around, he finds in his sights a woman sitting at a table with many candles lit on a shelf behind her.

As he keeps the gun on her, he looks around the room to make sure they are alone.

Jürgen now looks at the woman, "Who are you? Where am I? What town is this? Are you German? "

The woman calmly smiles and stands, all the while Jürgen follows her with his pistol.
"Young man, I am a woman and a mother. I know where I am, and I am more than German."
Confused by her answers Jürgen gets a bit agitated and starts to pace.

Before he can say a word the woman speaks again, "You may stay outside in the stable with the other beasts. Go now, for I have things to do."

Jürgen thinks to himself, "How dare this woman talk to me like this, I am SS! I should just..."

She looks at Jürgen and points, "Go now, I will call you back when I am ready."

Jürgen becomes enraged ... until he looks into her eyes, and he feels all his rage subside. The way she looks, and her demeanor reminds him of a woman he so loved ... his mother. He slowly opens the door and heads behind the house to the small stable.

As he enters the small stable, he sees there is only hay to lie on, and a few wool blankets that are neatly hung over the stable doors. Looking outside, he notices it's starting to snow. He should have just told that woman to go out to the cold stable, that's what a real SS soldier would have done.

Finding a warm corner, Jürgen takes off his backpack, sits down, and begins to look at what food he still has inside, besides his coveted chocolate bar. While he is glancing down, out of the corner of his eye, he sees movement underneath a haystack on the other side of the stable.

Jumping to his feet and pointing his weapon, he yells, "I saw you! Come out! Come out or I will shoot!"

With his eyes on the haystack he sees a small figure making its way out of the hay. Slowly the image begins to become clear in the almost dark stable. Jürgen notices a candle on a shelf, with one hand on his pistol; he reaches his other into his coat pocket, and pulls out a lighter. Lighting the candle, the image slowly reveals itself to be a small young girl, dressed entirely in rags, with the exception of a bright blue bow in her hair.

Jürgen walks over and stamps on the stack of hay to make sure she was the only one hiding. "Who are you? What is your name? Answer me! Now!" Jürgen's eyes and tone frighten the little girl and she backs into the corner. Jürgen again yells, "Speak to me! "

As the girls eyes tear over, a small voice speaks out, "I am Eliana".

Looking at her, Jürgen lowers his pistol, relaxes for a second, then grabs the girl and pulls up the sleeves on her ragged coat to reveal a tattoo. Throwing her to the ground, he yells, "Jüdin!" Looking down at the small figure scrambling back into the corner, Jürgen's hate begins to show in his eyes. After all her "kind" were responsible for killing his whole family two years ago.

He thinks to himself, "What sweet revenge". He points his pistol at the terrified little face. Now is his chance. He will have his first kill! He slowly puts his finger on the trigger and aims at her little head.

"Why do you hate me so" a little voice softly speaks out. Looking into her little frightened brown eyes, Jürgen pauses for a second. Along with the shiny blue ribbon in her hair, her little innocent eyes tear at his heart.

"This is a Jewish mind trick" he thinks to himself.
He again focuses on her, as the door swings open, and with it snowflakes blow in from outside. Before Jürgen can close the door, a small lamb rushes in, and positions itself between the girl and himself.

Now there are two sets of innocent eyes looking back at him. His mind is now totally confused, and he begins to pace.

He stops and barks at the little girl, "Where did you get that blue ribbon? "

Without hesitation the young girl replies, "First your name if you are going to shoot me, at least your name"

The young soldier surprised by the sudden boldness answers back, "Jürgen … now you! Where did you get it?"

"From the nice lady in the house, she said it was one of my presents. "

Jürgen is now totally confused, thinking to himself while pacing like a caged animal, "Now what? Oh what do I do? A Jüdin in my sights, and a lamb I could eat"

Looking down he watches the small four legged, big eyed, white ball of fur, lay down so tenderly between him and his "prey".

A gust of wind rocks the stable and an object falls from the rafters onto the hay. With a 'Ki-ting', Jürgen knows exactly what it is, a sound from happier times. Eliana and the lamb watch as the Luger is holstered and the fierce S.S. solider calmly walks over and picks up the guitar. Strumming it ever so lightly, only the high 'E' is out of tune, but is quickly tuned up.

Looking over at the two sets of innocent eyes looking at him, Jürgen calmly speaks, "I used to play since I was ten. I used to play at church. I...I remember how everyone came to see me play, during Christmas." Blowing on his cold finger tips to warm them up a bit; it did not take long before music filled the dimly lit stable. When Jürgen started to play his favorite song, 'Stille Nacht, Heilige Nacht', he could not resist singing along while playing. Within a few lyrics the little girl began to sing along. It was as if they had practiced to perform in front of an audience. As the two voices held the last note, calmness entered the shelter.

Looking at the young girl, "You say your name is Eliana?" The brown eyes just nod as a smile appears on the precious little face. "Eliana, where did you learn to sing that song?"

With an even a bigger smile, "It was the nice lady in the house, she sang it for me, just once ...but somehow I remembered it all" Looking a bit confused, the guitar player played a few more songs before gently laying the guitar down.

Jürgen just sat and stared at the two sets of brown eyes looking at him, one with a smile. Grabbing his backpack Jürgen reaches in and pulls out the first thing his fingers grab onto, his prized chocolate bar. Seeing a pair of eyes grow bigger, something comes over this heart that was once filled with so much hatred. Opening the wrapper, Jürgen breaks off a small piece, then hands the rest to those innocent eyes before him.

"Eliana, today is December 24th, I know Jewish people don't celebrate this, but it is custom to give a present, Merry Christmas"

The once fierce combat trooper sits back and watches as the little girl treasures every little morsel. This chocolate bar had been his prized possession, but his greatest pleasure was watching her eat it.

After she finished, she flashed the biggest smile he had ever seen, "Thank you, you are nice, not like the rest."

An emotion came over Jürgen; his hate was now dead and his compassion, alive.

He starts to think, "Why? How was it this little girl's fault ... the terrible thing that happened to my family? Before it happened, it always felt so good to play the guitar and sing in church".

A peace came over him, a feeling he had not had in two years. Seeing that the little girl was a bit cold, Jürgen grabbed a blanket and covered her and the lamb up. He then went and picked up the guitar and played, until the girl and lamb were fast asleep.

Now only the sound of two little snoring beings filled the stable as Jürgen closed his eyes … the first peace and serenity in two years.

It felt like hours had gone by when Jürgen opened his eyes to the sight of a little girl snuggled on his left, and a lamb on his right. He looked at his watch, still another half hour until Christmas day. His mind began to wander back to Christmas's past, and he could almost smell and taste the Pfefferkuchen.

As he was about to close his eyes again, a voice whispered harshly, "Quick you must go now, evil is at the doorsteps!'

Without hesitation the young soldier was up and looked out between one of the cracks in the stable wall. He could see two shadows drawing nearer across the moonlit open field. He grabbed his pocket size binoculars and tried to get a closer look. Just as he focused in, a shell blast in the distance lit up the sky, his view was clear … SS!

Thinking quickly, he wakes Eliana with his hand over her mouth and whispers, "We have to go, now, quietly."

Jürgen puts on his backpack, wraps Eliana up in a blanket and silently opens the door. As the two are almost out, their fury friend decides to tag along.

Smiling down at the two brown eyes, "You, little lamb, stay here; it's too dangerous for you."

With that, he scoots the lamb back with his feet and closes the door.

The former hate filled boy knows what will happen if they get caught, he cares not so much for himself, but his new little, innocent friend. Sneaking out, they try to stay in the shadows. If they can just stay amongst the shrubs, they can make it to the forest and be well hidden.

He now pays no attention to the weight on his back, nor in his arms. He moves like a cat on the prowl. The shrubs end about thirty yards from the forest. With the two shadows dressed in black, closing in, Jürgen makes a dash just as another shell explodes in the distance, revealing him and Eliana.

"Halt!!" a voice bellows out. Now the dash was on, only ten yards to go and…a loud shot and the boy's leg gives way and he, and his precious cargo, hit the snow. Within seconds the black wolves are upon them. One shines a flashlight on the two terrified souls looking up.

"You! You are an S.S. solider! Why are you running with this little girl?"

The other man walks over and instinctively pulls Eliana's sleeve up, while the light discloses the secret.
"Jüdin! You are trying to save this little Jüdin?"

Without hesitation a brave boy's voice barks back with the same tone, "Yes! She is my friend!"

The two S.S. men stare at the two on the ground, then at each other, and begin to laugh. One shoulders his rifle and pulls out his Luger. Jürgen begins to feel for his in the snow, but to no avail.

With a big grin on his face the beast with the Luger, laughs then clears his throat, "Stupid Boy, you have betrayed our code, for that you are condemned to death. But not until you see this filthy little Jüdin die before you!"

Cocking the pistol he aims at Eliana and fires, but not before Jürgen shields her little body with his.
As the bullet enters his body, he is enflamed with pain.

The other S.S. man draws his pistol, "Stupid Boy, well little Jüdin, you will both be food for the scavengers!"
Cocking his pistol, two loud shots echo through the night, and now two dead bodies lie in the snow, coloring it with a steaming red flow.

Footsteps can now be heard, as they hurriedly come closer to the two dead bodies.

A voice breaks the silence, "Hey Mac! Great shooting! …. Ya got both these swine-hunds, they're deader than dead!"

Eliana watches as more men in green uniforms surround her. Crawling over and hugging Jürgen she says softly, "Er ist mein Freund"

One of the G.I.'s calls over, "Hey Karl … come over here. I think this little girl is trying to tell us something in Kraut." The man comes over and Eliana tells him about Jürgen and how he is kind and saved her.

A man with a red cross on his helmet comes over and takes a look at the wounded boy before him. "Poor kid, he aint got much time, looks like a liver shot."

Karl translates this to Eliana, as tears fill her eyes.
Looking up, Jürgen smiles at Eliana, "Don't cry for me, you are safe, and I will be with my family soon."

Eliana takes off the blue bow that the lady had given her, and ties it around Jürgen's neck. "Merry Christmas my friend" Eliana now tells the translator that there is a house with only a lady inside, very close, and could they please take her friend there, out of the snow.

As tears fill her eyes, a few red eyed G.I.'s carry the critically injured savior to the house.

The G.I.'s knock, as the lady opens the door, "Sprichst du Deutsch?" Karl asks.

The lady smiles and answers in English, "I speak many languages".

The G.I.'s carry Jürgen in and tell the lady of his fate.
Laying him on a cot, Eliana again embraces her hero.
Jürgen cannot help but feel content with his actions.
A sudden blast in the distance and one man yells, "Grab the girl, let's go!"

Tears fall from those little brown eyes onto her friend, and he whispers out, "Go now and stay safe. Remember me when you're old and gray... I love you".
The little girl is carried away, and the boy's eyes close to darkness.

The lady kneels before him, watching the G.I.'s leave, "Go, I will take care of this, me, and my son in the stable."

Like sands in an hour glass, the years had passed in a
blink of an eye. Eliana had come back to Germany for her
granddaughters wedding. Seventy years have gone by.
It was once again Christmas Eve, as Eliana and her family
were driving along the German countryside. As the passed a
little town, a building caught her eye,
"Stop! We need to Stop!"

    Thinking that something must be wrong, her
granddaughters soon to be G.I. husband stopped the car.

    Eliana pointed, "There. Drive me there."

    As they pulled up Eliana gets out of the car, and walks to
the front of the building … getting ready to walk in.
"Grandma, what are you doing? That's a church, not a
Synagogue."

    Waving for all to follow, she enters and sits down.
Looking around she smiles, "I know this place, it did not look
like this, but the little house next door, is almost still the same."
Seeing the confused looks on her family's faces,
"I made a promise to a friend, a long, long time ago, I have not
forgotten…"

    A priest walks out and asks in German if he could help
them. He explains that Christmas Eve Mass would not be
until later that night, and they are getting ready to rehears for
it. Eliana explains she is from America but was here once as
a little girl, and she was just remembering a friend who died
here way back then.

    Looking into Eliana's brown eyes, full of sorrow, the Priest
smiles, and shakes his head "Yes".

As Eliana remembers that night so long ago, a guitar tunes up in the front corner of the church. It soon begins to play a familiar song, that she first heard that night in the stable, and has listened to every year since.
Back home in America it's called, Silent Night.

Eliana sings along quietly to the astonishment of her family. When finished, with a tear in her eye, she tells her family that she needs to go say thank you to the guitar player.

Waving at the Priest that let them stay to come over, she whispers to him, "Can I go up and thank the guitar player? That was so beautiful, and even though I am Jewish, this song touches my old heart."

"Of course! That is the best I have heard Father Johann play that song."

Eliana tells her family she will be right back and makes her way up front, scooting in behind Father Johann, she taps him on the shoulder and whispers,
"Thank you so much, you have made an old lady's life complete. I am Jewish but a nice boy once played this for me, and also saved me, on this night, seventy years ago."

Father Johann lays down his guitar and says, "She said I would see you again before I die. I never stopped believing."

As he slowly stands up and turns around, Eliana was stunned to see it was an old Priest that had played that song. Looking more closely she could see tears in his eyes.
Then around his white collar she saw something that made her eyes begin to flow as well.

A faded blue ribbon.

"Eliana! Eliana!" The two now embrace to the bewilderment of all in the church.

"Jürgen ...how? You died I remember"
They both sit down, arm in arm, as the now Father Johann tells the story,

"I remember you leaving ... darkness ... then light. Then the Lady and the Lamb were next to me. That is when I heard her say, 'Dear boy, don't worry, you will see her again before you die'. When I woke, the same soldiers were back and took me to a hospital. They called me a Christmas miracle."

Eliana still in shock, "So what became of the Lady? Did you see her again?"

Jürgen gets up and takes Eliana by the hand, "Come, I want to show you something."

Followed now by her family, Jürgen stops and points, "There ... when I rebuilt this church, I found her."

All are transfixed, for on the wall is a picture of the Lady from so long ago. Under the painting of her with a blue ribbon in her hair is a plaque that reads,

"Die Jungfrau Maria – The Virgin Mary"

The List

"Where is she? Please! Take me to her!"

Melissa is in a panic. She had just found out that her daughter had collapsed in the park next to their house, and had rushed to the hospital. Her best friend Kate had been watching her daughter while Melissa was finishing up that last bit of Christmas shopping on that fateful morning of December 24th.

Having made it to St. Mary's in record time, she is running down the hallway, as Kate and a nurse see her, and rush toward the distraught mother. The nurse stops Melissa from going any further.

"I'm sorry you can't go in there. The doctors are doing all they can. Please go with your friend to the waiting area and as soon as I hear any news whatsoever, I promise you, I will give you the details."

Kate puts her arm around her crying friend as her eyes too swell up, as they walk down the Christmas decorated hallway.

Melissa looks at Kate, "This could be it. I knew this day would come sometime, but oh please … God not on this day, please."

Kate embraces her friend, "Mel, keep the faith, it's all we can do, Kammi is in the best hands she can possibly be in. Now we just need some help from above. Come; let's go sit down in the waiting room. They'll let us know the second they find something out."

Any other time the Christmas décor would have cheered a person up a bit, but not today this Hawaiian Christmas Eve.

Kammi is an energetic little girl with pigtails and a heart of gold. She approaches everything in life with a smile. Yet it is that heart of gold of hers that's the problem. A few years back when she was five, this now seven year old, found out that she had a chronic heart disease that nothing short of a transplant could cure. This didn't stop Kammi one bit as the little Hawaiian Princess only added to all the beauty that surrounds her. Each day she rose up and went on her little adventures along the beach near her home. Wanting to be, "independent", Melissa agreed to let her go out and play, as long as she had her 'Life Alert' necklace on and called her mother every half hour or so, which she always did. Kammi understood that all that was before her, may be gone in an instant, so she made the best of what life has to offer … each and every day.

Kate, a former teacher, would come over five days a week and home school Kammi, to give her more "independent" time to explore the majestic island to her heart's desire.

Now Kate and Melissa, both clearly distraught, open the door to the waiting area to find four other worried people sitting inside.

One is a slender girl who appears to be in her late teens or early twenties. Another an older woman in her seventies, followed by one man with a cane who looks to be in his thirties. And finally a chair occupied by an older, longhaired, Hawaiian surfer.

Melissa and Kate take a seat on the opposite side of the room with a coffee table between them and the other group of people. Looking at the others, Melissa and Kate can tell that they too are clearly troubled. The Christmas lights are twinkling, yet the only sound in the room is the ticking of the clock on the wall. Minutes seem like an eternity for those waiting for some news of their loved ones.

The young girl breaks the silence as the ticking of the clock just kept getting louder. "Hi, I'm Karen, I'm sorry to break the silence, but I have to just let it all out. I can't just sit here and think. I'm here for a friend that I call Sis. I don't have a sister, but if I did, this one would be the greatest. Sis has been helping me with my dog, Fanny. You see Fanny got really sick and Sis would come and watch her while I would run documents to the law office. I work from home, and I'm lucky my boss is a dog person and understands. Sis sits with Fanny, pet her, and makes her feel loved when I am gone. Sis always tells me to have faith, and all will be alright. Just when I was ready to lose all hope, she said, 'Christmas miracles happen you know'. And they did! This morning Fanny was up and about just like before she got sick. I was just about to take her for a checkup when I was told Sis was in the hospital. So, here I am and here I'll be until I find out what's going on."

Karen leans back in her chair as the man with the cane leans forward. With a voice of authority he starts, "My name is Tanner, U.S. Marine Corp, retired. I met Private T.C. last summer on the beach. I would roll out there daily in my wheelchair, look into the waves, and think back to what it was like to walk the beach with my wife. I was wounded in Iraq by a roadside bomb, and lost the use of my legs. I became a bitter man, and cursed God. Let's just say I became a full blown atheist. My actions of hate and anger over my situation drove my wife and many of my friends away. Then one summer morning, Private T.C. came walking up. Private T.C. explained to me that life can take you where you really don't want to be, and believe you me, I was there. Private T.C. also had some medical issues, but always had faith. Never giving up on me, T.C. brought my faith back and abolished my hate and anger. T.C. was always telling me to 'keep the faith'. This morning I stood up, grabbed the cane that Private T.C. had made for me, and walked along the beach for the first time in years. Then a friend of Private T.C.'s came running and told me that T.C. had an accident and that I must hurry. Now all I can do is sit here and pray. That is all."
Leaning back the rest of the group can clearly see that Tanner is praying for Private T. C. on the inside.

The older woman now scoots forward, and with a shaky raspy voice she starts, "Trudy …, I'm here for Trudy. My name is Grace. Unfortunately at my age, many of my friends are gone. I live in the house that my late husband Carl built shortly after World War Two. At that time, the house was out in the middle of nowhere. But progress made its way closer and closer each and every year. Soon we were surrounded by many big and fancy places."

"Over the years, Carl and I got offers to sell ... but this was 'our place', and now it's my place ... full of a lifetime of treasured memories. My friend Trudy would come over and have tea with me, and I would tell her about how things used to be on the island. It was truly a paradise. But since Carl passed, my house taxes have gotten higher and higher. The last time Trudy came over, I told her that's it ... I have to sell. I'm out of money. As we both sat there, I could see tears coming down her once smiling face, as she asked if there's anything I could do. Nothing short of a miracle or a winning lottery ticket I told her. Well I'll be, Trudy reached into her bag and pulled out a dollar, telling me to have faith and buy that ticket. So I did, and last night I won the jackpot. I was hoping to see Trudy today, but was told she was here, and it's not looking good. I want to thank her and make sure she never has to worry in her life again ... and now I just worry about her life." Scooting back a somber look comes over the elderly woman as her thoughts are with her friend, Trudy.

The longhaired surfer looking man is just looking out the window, and seems to be mesmerized with the palm trees decorated in Christmas lights.

After a few seconds he turns and looks at the others, "My name is Charlie. They used to call me 'Waves' back in the eighties, because I would surf them all man. I even won a few surf competitions in Australia's monsters. Then one day, the biggest kahuna waves ever came forth, and I had to surf them no matter what the risk. I wiped out super hard and was under for a while, until they finally snatched me back up out of the water. Seems I hit my board so hard, it caused me to go blind. Yeah all the sympathy came in and all that support crap for a short time, but then Waves was gone with the tide."

"They should have let the waters take me. All I had left was a small condo a few blocks from the waves. I had no one that wanted to hang with me. And then one day, I was playing my guitar on my patio, under my lemon trees and feeling the warm sun on my face … when I heard someone tapping along with a pair of sticks. When I asked who was there they said, 'just call me Jams'. Soon Jams would come by and tap along as I played, which was cool. But what I really wanted was just to sit at the beach and feel the waves. So Jams took me there man, like at least three times a week. Jams is way cool, and always has a positive attitude. Man, I told Jams that I appreciated everything. Then I found out, Jams didn't even play with real sticks, just plain ole tree sticks. So when Jams came by yesterday, I had ordered a pair of real sticks as a present. I said, 'I wish I could have seen the look on your face.' Jams just said 'keep the faith brother, keep the faith'. So, if I seem distracted by all this stuff around me, well … by faith, or miracle or just Jams' encouragement, I opened my eyes this morning and things slowly came into focus. What a far-out crazy experience. How the world has changed since the eighties. I was waiting for Jams when a pretty lady told me something bad happened, and Jams ended up here. It totally bummed me out, man. I've never even seen Jams face but I will for sure be keeping the faith, and I'll wait to see that face … I will man, I will."

Melissa and Kate sit there, still numb as they listen to these stories. Melissa also wants to open up, but her emotions are getting the best of her. Feeling guilty that the others may be here for their loved friends, her only thoughts are on her little Kammi.

The others take notice, and the room again becomes silent, as those there are deep in their own thoughts. Minutes seem to be like hours again. A nurse is seen approaching and comes up to Melissa.

"Here this was on Kammi when they brought her in. And no, there is no news yet."

Handing Melissa a big white bag, Melissa sees Kammi's backpack inside. Pulling it out, she looks at Kate, and again begins to sob while laying the backpack on the coffee table. Glancing over at the others Melissa notices Karen, Grace and Tanner looking at her with the same looks on their faces.

Out of nowhere Grace blurts out, "What are you doing with Trudy's bag?"

Followed by Karen, "No that's Sis's backpack".

Tanner's distinguished voice barks out, "Private Tough Cookies survival pack".

Melissa and Kate's eyes open wide, as the once blind surfer just stares at everyone. Feeling something inside, Melissa unzips the backpack and pulls out a pair of new drumsticks.

The surfer breaks down and begins to cry.

Melissa and Kate look at each other in disbelief.

Melissa looks at Grace, "Why did you call her Trudy?" Wiping her eyes with a tissue Grace looks at Melissa, "because she reminds me so much of a friend long ago. Please forgive me."

Melissa and Kate are in a state of awe as they both realize, Kammi had touched all of these people's lives.

Laying the drumsticks upon her lap, Melissa sees a piece of paper in the backpack and pulls it out. As she begins to look at it, the flood waters from her eyes begin.

Reading it, she lays it down on the little coffe table for all to see. It reads:

My Christmas list
By Kammi Louwane

5. I want Karen's dog Fanny to be all better.

4. I want Miss Grace to stay in her house for ever and ever.

3. I want Sergeant Tanner to walk the beach again.

2. I want Charlie Waves to see again and surf the waves.

1. I want mommy to be happier than happy forever.

No toys for me Santa, just this please

The room is soon filled with sobs and tears flowing from all eyes. So much so, that they don't see the doctor with the somber look on his face approaching. As he opens the door all eyes are upon him and all ears are listening.

Clearing his throat, he looks at Melissa, "Maybe I should ask the others to leave."

Melissa knowing what is about to be said will affect all those present, "No doctor, we are all family here thanks to Kammi. Say what needs to be said."

Looking up at the ceiling, the doctor is trying to keep his composure, "Kammi is slipping away. Only a heart transplant can save her now. I checked to see if any donor hearts were available, but there are none."

A teary eyed surfer blurts out, "Take mine Doc! Take mine!" In unison the rest also repeat the same phrase.

Raising his hands, "Please, this is a tough thing. All your hearts even if you wanted to give them are too big or too old. I can call down to the chapel to have a priest give last rites if you wish. I am so sorry".

The room is now filled with sobbing people, as the doctor's phone rings. As he answers it, all eyes are again upon him.

"Yes, what? What do you mean? Look that can't be …who told you that? Nurse? What nurse? We have no nurse by that name in this hospital! I'll be right there!" Looking at all with a shocked expression, "I should ask you all to stay here, but something's telling me that you should follow me!"

As the doctor hurries down the Christmas lit hallway, he is eagerly followed by an entourage.

With Melissa and Kate in the lead they all follow the rushing doctor who waves off the oncoming nurses, "They're all with me!"

Entering the room they see Kammi sitting up and a nurse at her side.

"See, I told you doctor! When I entered the room, the other nurse was leaving and said all is better."

Looking at the EKG monitor it shows everything is normal. Rubbing his face, "I don't understand."

Kammi looks at the astonished guests, "Hi Mommy, Hi Aunt Kate. Hello Karen, Miss Grace, Sergeant Tanner, and Waves. What are you all doing here?"

They're all speechless, as the doctor begins to think. "Wait a second, how did you others know that Kammi was here, when you all arrived within seconds of her even arriving? All of you …arrived … before …" looking at Melissa and Kate, "You two! The mother and the friend."

Waves speaks up, "Man like I said before a pretty lady told me."

Grace also comments, "I was at the store when a pretty lady told me."

Tanner quickly jumps in, "I was approached at the beach by a pretty lady."

Karen too confirms a pretty lady.

Now all are just staring at each other when Kammi breaks the silence.

"I was just lying there and suddenly I opened my eyes. The most beautiful lady nurse was holding my hand. She said that I'm all better now, and not to worry …so are my friends and my mommy."

The doctor looks at Kammi, "Kammi, did this nurse by chance have a name?"

Kammi begins to think, "Well she said her little boy really appreciates a person full of love and unselfishness. One day she said I would meet him and… Mary, she said her name was Mary! Can I get something to eat now, I'm hungry."

Six souls were forever changed on this Hawaiian Christmas Eve…

I guess the only thing left to say is,

Mele Kalikimaka

Homo Incognitus Redit

(The Stranger Returns)

Part 2 of 'The Trilogy'

Sara stood there looking across the half frozen river, on that cold overcast afternoon of December 24th 1883.
The skies had just opened their icy flood gates and released beautiful flakes from the Heavens. Sara watched as many fell softly and accumulated, while others were doomed to melt in the still unfrozen flowing waters of the river. How quickly their existence dissipated into nothingness. A few more steps out, and the thin ice would give way, and she too, would just wash away.

Thinking back through her twenty three year life; it had been one of great ups and devastating downs. Her father was a frontiersman, gold miner, and turned scout for the army out west. Her mother was a Lakota, daughter of a great chief. While growing up she often had fond memories of life on the great open plains, along with the millions of great buffalos that once roamed freely. Her mother died of the fever when she was twelve; her father became distraught and began working more to escape the sorrowful pain caused by this devastating loss. Sara saw less and less of her father, waiting endless hours for his return to their home at the fort. He had a small wooden box, which he had made, and often times told Sara, "Soon, you'll never need to worry again."

Then in the summer of 1876, he perished as one of the scouts for the 7th Calvary under George Armstrong Custer.

Sara received a letter a few days before his demise, in which he told of the enemy's great force. He knew this would be his last ride due to the deaf ears of their commander. The once "Never Worry Box" was now gone, and all Sara had left was a bear claw silver necklace that once belonged to her Lakota grandfather.

Sara had learned to cook and clean, and as the railroad came through, a town was built near the fort. It was there that she met a young handsome, man of the railroad. His family had invested in the "Iron Horse", and John was along to keep tabs on their investments. When they first met, John could not keep his eyes off of the nineteen year old beauty, nor she off the twenty four year old financier. A romance ensued, and soon there was a little boy, John Junior. Sara ran a place in town that provided food and washed the clothes of the railroad workers, who became the new tenants of the town, while John kept moving with the rails westward expansion.

In the summer of 1883, John was summoned back east to his family home, and he of course wanted to take John Junior with him. At first Sara hesitated, but sadly gave in. John Junior was all she really had in her life. Before leaving Sara gave John Junior the bear claw necklace for good luck,

"Mother loves you, be good for your father and I'll see you very soon. When you miss me, just rub the bear claw and I'll be right there in your heart, always."

The summer turned to fall and Sara began to worry as only a few letters had arrived from John, promising he and their son would be back soon. Sara was thinking about taking the railroad east, as her business and the town had dried up as people were moving further west. Without warning, a telegram arrived, and Sara was once again devastated by the worst news life can bear. It was a message from John … John Junior had died of fever. John was also devastated. So much so, that he was leaving the country to help build railroads for the British in India.

Sara now had nothing, and no one.

"Just a few more steps out, then this burning pain in my heart will be over quickly." Sara's thoughts were now in control.

Taking a few steps out, as snowflakes gently melted on her saddened face, Sara was ready for the end. She stopped as a strange tapping noise filled tranquil moment. Off to her right, a man was walking along the frozen river very close to the thin ice. Adjusting her eyes to the strange sight, she notices a man with long white hair, a cane, and darkened spectacles.

A thought races through her mind," Oh my God a blind man, he's going to fall in!" Sara backs up to the bank, "Hey! Mr. Stop! You're on thin ice! Don't move an inch, I'm coming for you!" Sara rushes down the river bank and reaches the stranger. The man stopped and smiled, looking at Sara.

"Well howdy! I hear you breathing as if you were just running or something. I heard you yell … what kinda mess did I get myself into now?"

Catching her breath, "Mr. Please listen to me and do exactly what I say, I can't come guide you as you are on thin ice. The river below you is very deep, and the current very fast. Turn to your left, listen to my voice, and slowly walk this way."

Getting a confused look on his face the white haired blind stranger calmly clears his throat, "Well, I have been on thin ice in the past, but never literally." As his smile returns the man slowly turns towards Sara, "Well, okay here I come, hope I don't go for a frozen dip, as I don't know how to swim."

Sara nervously starts talking the stranger towards her, while the crackling noise below his feet puts her nerves to the test. With what seems like forever, the man finally makes it close enough to where Sara can grab his arm and lead him safely to the bank of the river. Helping him up the slope to flat ground, Sara sees the man has nothing but a cane, a small backpack, and a coat, which was not made for the winter cold.

She asks the stranger, "What in God's name are you doing wandering about out here in the middle of nowhere? Are you blind AND crazy? Had you fallen into the river, you would have frozen to death tonight."

Adjusting his backpack, the white haired blind man shakes his head up and down, smiles, "Boy oh boy you're right. You see I was on the train, heading east, when, well by golly, I took a wrong turn and tumbled off the train. I had walked quite a ways and then, well, I guess I heard an angel giving me directions to stop. Could this angel take me somewhere warm, and maybe let me purchase a meal? I am a bit hungry too."

Sara just shakes her head in disbelief, "Alright mister …
hey, what's your name?"

Tapping Sara gently on the leg with his cane with a smile
he replies, "Mister will be just fine, as blind men can't leave
their mark anyway. I am really hungry."

Sara now gets a smile, "well then 'Mister I'm Hungry', I'll
take you to my place for a bite, we still have a depot, but with
Christmas coming tomorrow, the train won't be by for a few
days." Sara starts to lead the smiling stranger along and
takes a look back at the half frozen river. A strange warm
feeling comes over her as she hangs on to the strangers arm,
thinking, "Something good must come of this, for two lives
were almost lost."

As the two walk into town a man with a camera sees
them, "Hey, good afternoon, ready for a special picture, after
all it's almost Christmas?"

Sara whispers to her blind stranger, "He's gonna charge
us, he's on his last leg here in this town."

With a big smile her new friend whispers back, "let me
chat with him". Walking over to the man with the big camera
on a tripod, the blind man exchanges a few words and walks
back to Sara, "Alright, all set … take the picture."

The man sets up the camera and snaps the picture with a
smoky flash. Pulling out his pocket watch, "Your print will be
ready in an hour and a half." Picking up the bulky box and
stand the man rushes off to his shop.

The darkened spectacles look toward Sara, still smiling, "Well my dear, an hour and a half is just about time to fill this old blind man's hungry pit." Sara just chuckles and leads the man to her place, the whole way along, a feeling of comfort comes over her, as if she started anew, with all her emotional pain gone.

Sara leads the man in, takes his coat and backpack, and seats him at the table. Throwing a few logs into the cast iron stove, the warmth soon fills the place. Having a small bottle of brandy she pours her new friend a shot. "Here you go Mister, this and the stove will warm you in a flash."

Taking a sip, "Wow, that's good, almost as good as one I had with a short French general once upon a time".

Sara begins to fix a stew while the stranger sits and smiles. He begins to whistle a nice little tune. The melody catches Sara's ear, "What an enchanting little tune, seems like it was made for this day."

Stopping with a big smile, "Yeah, that's what they said in Austria." Beginning again where he left off, the tune fills Sara's place with a touch of Christmas joy.

Having finished cooking, Sara fills up the strangers plate a few times before he kindly motions he's full. "No more, I feel I'll burst like a cannon"

Getting up the stranger puts on his coat and backpack, I'll be right back. I'm going to get our picture."

Sara shakes her head, "You don't even know where you're going, how can you get our picture?"

Opening the door and looking back at Sara, dark glasses mirroring the snowflakes outside, "Madame, just because I am blind doesn't mean I don't know where to go. I turn right, go forty paces, and turn left go about ten paces till the stairs, walk up four stairs, take two steps and knock on the door.
Blind yes, but I still know where to go."

Again a chuckle comes out of Sara, "Oh yeah, then how did you almost end up in the river?"

Snickering back at Sara, "Only you Sara, know the answer to that".

Closing the door Sara watches out her window as the blind stranger with long white hair walks the path of which he had spoken of. Opening her front door, Sara watches as he gets to the top of the stairs, enters the photography shop and shuts the door.

Sara starts cleaning the dishes when a thought hits her, "Wait a second, I never told that man my name, how did he know to call me Sara?"
Finishing the dishes, Sara thinks the man should be back by now. Putting on her coat she walks out the door, down to the photographers place and walks in the front door. Seeing no one around the place, Sara speaks loudly, "Hello? Is there anybody here?"

A few seconds later the photographer opens a door and steps out, "Here ya go Sara, all framed with glass on top, just got it done."

Baffled Sara looks at the man, "where's my friend?
I saw him enter about a half hour ago."

Now the man looks baffled, "Umm, no, no one has come in this afternoon but you. He told me that you would come pick it up when he paid me early this morning."

Sara shakes her head, "This morning? But I just found him on the ice at the river this afternoon."

Throwing his hands up in the air, "I don't know nothing about no river, and oh, he also said to give you this, let me get it ... it's a tad heavy."
Walking into the other room the photographer retrieves a wooden box. Sara's eyes are brought to tears as she recognizes the box.

With a shaky voice Sara softly says, "Thank you"
Grabbing the box and framed picture, Sara turns to leave,

"Hold on Sara, he told me to tell you to keep Christmas in your heart, and one day all the riches you have ever desired will be yours. I have no clue what he meant, but there you go."

Sara slowly walks away and makes it back to her place setting the heavy wooden box and picture on the table. Unlatching the box, Sara's eyes glow, as inside, it is filled with twenty dollar gold pieces. Sara will never have to worry again, just like her father once said.

****
****
****

The Great War had been raging for three years before the American Doughboys began to arrive. It was Christmas Eve, 1917, and the trenches were rife with fighting.

Flying just above them J.P. thought, "Those poor guys stuck down in those freezing holes; at least I get a warm bed at night." Having left that morning in his plane, J.P. was one of the privileged fighters, as his family had money and he did benefit from it.

J.P. never really knew his real father as his parents divorced, and his mother took J.P. along when she moved to Europe with her new husband. Growing up, J.P. remembered all the fancy parties at the elaborate estates, and dinners, and traveling first class on trains and ships. But it was a specific ship that changed his life. Being a first class passenger always had its benefits, but that night, J.P is certain only his "Luck Charm" had saved him. He turned fifteen that April 14th night and had just celebrated his birthday when the ship, HMS Titanic, hit an iceberg. His mother and step dad did not survive the infamous night.

Heading back to Europe, J.P. found out that only a small trust fund had been set up for him. He had just enough money to get into a brand new and exclusive school for aviation. Flying solo by 1914, the outbreak of World War One, called his name. Being an American citizen, he had to volunteer with the French Flying Corp. For three years he had waited for his country to join the fight. During this time he had seen many of his friends perish in the dogfights above the trenches. Having sent many a Hun down in flames, J.P. is one of the very few that has lasted without a scratch.

But things change, and that Christmas Eve morning the young fighter pilot began to worry. No, not about the weather as it was an unusually warm December morning when he took to the skies, but two days before he had lost his "Lucky Charm", somewhere over the trenches during an intense dogfight. It had always been with him since he could remember.

Checking the skyline for German planes, as he has done for years now, J.P. gets a knot in his stomach for the very first time. Searching the skies for his adversary, a German pilot named Helmut ... who had just as many kills as the American, and the same amount of experience.

"Today would not be a good day to run into Helmut" J.P. is thinking as a group of dots appear on the horizon. "Damn, well, today may be my last day!" he thinks out loud as the German planes start to close in. Behind them something else grabs J.P.'s attention ... a massive front of darkening clouds. Already feeling the temperature dropping in his open air cock pit, two things were not in the favor of this World War One pilot.

J.P. could now see the markings of Helmut's plane, as Helmut could also see the Americans. Breaking off from the rest of their groups, these two knights of the sky, head for their winner take all joust amongst the darkening clouds. Both heading toward each other, their machine guns spitting out flames in the ever colder freezing air. One pass, J.P. did not manage a hit, nor did Helmut. Both turn and head against each other again, but before J.P. or Helmut can fire a single shot, a strong wind unlike either had ever felt before, sent both wooden planes toppling towards the ground.

J. P. fought with all his might to pull up, but he was in a tailspin. "Well, this is it, not by a Hun, but by Mother Nature". As the ground rapidly approaches, J.P. is now in a cold sweat pulling with all his remaining strength. At the last possible second, the plane straightens out just enough for J.P. to land before his flap cables snap along with his biplanes wing. Rolling a hundred yards, the Knights steed comes to rest in some overgrown thickets.

J.P. slowly climbs out, as a wall of wind, cold, and snow descends upon him. Making out a church steeple in the distance, J.P. makes it inside just as the whiteout blizzard hits. Looking around, he realizes it's a very old church, somewhere in "no man's land" between the two conflicting armies. Shaking off the snow, J.P. is just about ready to sit down on the old wooden benches, when the door fly's open. Blinded by the whiteness filling the doorway, J.P has to adjust his eyes as a shadowy figure appears. Within a few seconds J.P. recognizes what's before him and draws his Colt 1911, while the other figure does the same with his Luger.

Both cock their weapons at the same time and fire, to no avail. J.P. tries again as does Helmut, but with the same results. Both throw down their pistols, and grab their survival knives and advance toward each other. They get within a few yards of each other when loud, "Crack!" echoes through the small abandoned church.

Both men are startled and turn toward the loud noise. Standing there is a man with long white hair, dark sunglasses, and a cane firmly stretched out in front of him flat on a wooden bench.

"Nicht in der Kirche!!! Not In the Church!"

Stopping in their tracks the two adversaries lower their knives. Staring in their direction the white haired man speaks in German again, then again in English, "Isn't there enough killing done already? Do you have to kill on this Holiest of nights? If you wish to, do it outside! Or put your weapons away and sit!"

J.P looks at the enemy just a few yards away, a man who has killed many of his friends. Looking into Helmut's eyes, he can tell, the Hun is thinking the same thing. Lowering and sheathing their knives, both men sit down a few pews apart, wary of each other. The white haired stranger raises his cane and taps his way to the pew in between them. J.P. starts to get a feeling of shame inside, something he has never felt.

Looking at the stranger between them, "I'm sorry, are you the priest of this place?"

A big smile appears on the strangers face, "no, not exactly, do me a favor … darkness is moving in. I can feel there are no candles lit. Take these matches and light them please. I want to make sure you two can keep an eye on each other, so I don't have to."

Flashing a quick smile, the stranger hands some matches to J.P. while assuring Helmut that all is good. J.P. lights all the candles and returns to his pew.
Fluffing up his white long hair a bit, the stranger asks Helmut to go to the front of the church and retrieve his bag.
Retrieving the bag Helmut gives it to the waiting hands and returns to his seat, a bit stunned as well.

Reaching into the long bag, "Oh, my, I was going to save this until tomorrow, but, since I won't be going anywhere till this storm passes, here we go." Pulling out a loaf of bread and a round cheese still encased in wax.
"Wait, wait … Ah! There it is"

The stranger pulls out a bottle of wine. Both airmen stare at the smiling figure before them. Asking for a knife in both languages, both men eagerly offer the stranger their former weapons. The blind man takes them both.

"One is for the bread and one for the cheese. See? You two can work together. Before we eat, are you Catholic?" Both men nod yes.
"Then, we will need to do communion first."
Smiling he reaches into the bag pulls out an old looking challis. Opening the wine, he then breaks off two pieces of crust.

Speaking in Latin, the man begins to perform the ritual when J.P. clears his throat, "Uh … so you ARE a Priest?"

The man turns and smiles "Close enough, now hush". Completing the communion, the man feeds and gives drink to the two prior combatants.

After the bread, cheese, and last bit of wine is gone the man reaches into the bag and pulls out a guitar, telling both his onlookers to sit back and relax. The blind stranger plays and sings songs in both languages, finishing with his favorite in German, which J.P., having lived in Europe most of his life, has heard and knows.

All three sing along as the candles begin to burn low. J.P. thinks to himself, he has never felt so at ease, even five feet from the man he tried to kill earlier. Sitting back, the white-haired stranger becomes the interpreter for the two men and all laugh it up for what seems to be hours.

Looking at the white-haired blind stranger, J.P. says, "You know, I lost my good luck charm a few days ago, and I thought for sure as I was tumbling toward the ground, that this was the end. I somehow now know that I was spared for a good reason."

Touching J.P.'s hand, "You never know what the Good Lord has in store for you today, tomorrow, or years from now. But I got a feeling good luck is with you, no matter what." The white-haired stranger then has a short conversation with Helmut in German, and picks up his guitar and begins to play again. As he joyfully plays, J.P and Helmut both stand, and shake hands and wish each other, a Merry Christmas.

Both men sit back, close their eyes, and let the enchanting melodies of the guitarist take them away.

It was daylight when both finally awoke to find the white-haired blind stranger gone. Both call out for him, but all they get is silent echoes. Both men again stand, salute each other and shake hands. As J.P. reaches into his pocket he feels something. Pulling it out, he sees that it's a picture in a small frame. In the picture is a pretty woman and a young girl. "What is this?" as he takes a closer look at the photograph. Helmut begins saying something to J.P. Not knowing what he is saying J.P. shows the picture to Helmut, who sheepishly gestures to put it in his hand.

Saying a few words, he points to the picture, then to his heart. J.P then knows that this is Helmut's wife and little girl, a part of killing you don't think about.

"Danke, Danke!" Helmut says as he puts it into his shirt pocket, over his heart. But before he can put in in all the way, he has to pull something out … some kind of trinket.

"My Good Luck Charm!" J.P. cries out happily. He then points to it and HIS heart.

Neither man knew how this all came to be on that Christmas Eve and Christmas Day of 1917, but they mysteriously got back something that they both cherished.

The two never had to fight each other again as the French moved in and Helmut became a P.O.W. But the friendship continued as J.P. visited Helmut many times on leave and taught him English, while he in turn, learned German. After the war the two became good friends and even visited each other in their lands. Both landed jobs in the aviation fields. J.P. became a great designer, yet always looked back at that Christmas Eve as a changing point in his life.

Helmut too had accomplished many things. But one thing he would never know. Helmut saved a drowning boy after the war, and in his mind that was the reason he was spared that Christmas of 1917. Just an unknown at the time, the boy was Oskar Schindler … but that's another story.

****
****
****

It has been two months since what became known as Black Tuesday on October 24th 1929 hit the nation. The December chill had moved in, and Christmas Eve was not what it once was, especially for Jack.

Loading six rounds into the cylinder of an old revolver; the forty nine year old man started thinking back on how he got into this desperate situation. He never had to worry about anything; he was always taken care of as a young boy, traveling, exotic trips, the best that life had to offer, … never a dull moment. As he grew into a young man he learned the business side of life, after he inherited his father's wealth upon his death. Jack invested the majority of his fortune in the new stock market and made millions, the rest he stashed away into banks. Having married four times, he only cared about himself, even when his first wife left, with their child, he just moved on. Every day was a best of the best day, with the best of everything. Whether it was food, drink, living, cars, or women, always the best for Jack. Then came Black Tuesday … the day the Market crashed, and millions with it.

Waking up the day after Black Tuesday, Jack had lost his fortune. The banks had failed and his money was gone. Even the money he had in his once plush penthouse apartment was gone, as his newest 'former wife' had cleaned out the safe. He had a few hundred dollars in his wallet, and an old pocket watch, and that's all that remained. Jack went to all his former business partners and financial advisors, but was turned away without a word. Somehow they all had gotten wind of the crash, and cashed in on the market just in the nick of time, leaving Jack as the sacrificial lamb.

They even mocked him, when he was on the streets as they drove by in their chauffeured cars, pointing and laughing.

Standing in the alley, Jack knew those who had misguided him, would gather for a traditional Christmas party at the Executives Club just down the street. All who had been villains would perish, five of his former partners, and himself. For one thing Jack now realized, after having lived on the streets and being shunned by all those he once mingled with, he could have done so much good for all the people who had little. Those poor souls who had nothing, and struggled each and every day.

Sticking his revolver in his pocket, Jack takes a deep breath, looks towards the heavens as small flakes of snow begin gently fall, "I'm sorry God. If you're real, you know how bad of a human I have been. It's going to get worse with what I must now do … please forgive me".
Soon his life of always searching for happiness will be over. Jack slowly steps out of the alley and walks towards his destiny.

"Funny", he thinks, "this area is nothing but run down slums, yet three blocks down, the millionaires relax in their dwellings."
Passing an alley, Jack is startled by a scuffle. Stopping, he notices four unpleasant men roughhousing with what appears to be a man hanging on to a long bag. Upon closer observation, Jack notices the man has a cane, dark sunglasses and long white hair. "What the…These hoodlums are trying to take a blind man's possessions?"

Jack stops and takes a few steps into the alley, "Hey!, leave that guy alone!" He is ignored as one man rips the blind man's shirt. Jack steps closer, "Scumbags! Did you hear me! Leave that man alone!"

Suddenly all four draw their attention towards Jack. The biggest and harshest looking of the bunch looks at Jack, "Move on, mind your own business, or you'll suffer the consequences!"

Jack stands up straight, stares down the man, "Let him go now, or deal with me!"

With the blind man on the ground the four start to move toward Jack. The harsh hoodlum snarls, "I warned you fool, now ya gonna bleed!"

All four whip out knives and advance on Jack. For a second a bolt of fear hits Jack, until he feels his coat pocket. The four rush towards Jack as he pulls out the revolver "BANG! BANG! BANG! BANG! BANG! BANG!" the shots ring out.

When the smoke clears, the blind man speaks up, "nice shooting partner."

Jack looks over and see's the blind man getting to his feet, "What do you mean nice shooting? I missed them all and they ran off!"

The blind man adjusts his glasses, "I mean great shooting, that you missed me!" Displaying a huge smile, "I owe ya one sheriff".

Jack walks over and picks up the cane and bag, handing them to the stranger before him. Looking at the strangers ripped shirt, "Well looks like all they got away with was a piece of cloth, you alright otherwise?"

Brushing himself off, "Oh yeah, fine and dandy, but now I need to change my shirt"

Jack smiles at the man, and a warm feeling comes over him, as if something had been lifted off his tormented shoulders. Grabbing Jacks arm the stranger faces Jack, "Look friend, I wish I could buy you dinner or something for your help, I have a few dollars … what do you say?"

Jack pats the man on his back, "No, you keep your money; I know how things now are."

Smiling even a bigger smile, the longhaired blind man says, "I tell you what, there's a place just down the street, with a gray haired lady they all call Mother Christmas … she has been serving food on Christmas Eve for years and years, please join me for a bite and some conversation.
Let me get to know the man who saved me."

Jack gets a smirk, "Mister, you would not like the man who saved you.   I have done some awful things in my life."

Tapping Jack with his cane, "Yet today, you did something good, it's a start."

Jack looks at the smile before him and thinks, "Well, I came for revenge and to end it all, only had six bullets, and now I feel totally humbled by a blind man. Maybe, this is a step towards redemption."

Giving Jack a swat with his cane, "Now if you would do me one more favor. I'm going to go change my shirt as I live just down the alley ... here take this coin and could you please call a friend and tell him I'll be at Mother Christmas's place? I have not seen my old friend in a while"

How could Jack refuse the gentle man's words, "Okay no problem, who's your friend and what's his number. There's a phone booth around the corner. What's the message and where is Mother Christmas's place? I'm getting a bit hungry now myself"

After taking the coin and the info, Jack starts to walk out of the alley, looking back, "Hey, are you going to be safe enough? I mean those guys may return."

Turning with a smile, "Jack, I'll be just fine, remember we have a date, I have to at least look presentable. You know it is Christmas Eve and miracles do happen."

The blind man turns and walks away. Jack has a smile on his face ... something he has not had in a while. Walking a few steps out of the alley, Jack hears the man whistling a tune. Thinking for a second, "Hey, I know that song!" Getting a puzzled look on his face Jack looks back down the alley as the man disappears into a building, "Hey, did I tell him my name?"

Jack stops off and makes the call for his new friend, relaying the message, then walks the few blocks down to Mother Christmas's place. Looking in the window he notices benches and tables like those he had seen in pubs in Europe. Not a lot of people, with it being almost four o'clock.

Walking in Jack is greeted by a gray haired lady rushing up to meet him with a big smile, "Hello stranger, I am Mother Christmas! At least that's what they have come to call me on this day over the years. The rest of the year, I am just Miss Walker. Welcome, what is your name?"

Jack gets a comfortable feeling, something he has not had since he was a young child. Smiling back at the cheerful woman he responds, "Hi, I'm Jack, it's a pleasure to meet you Mother Christmas."

Reaching out his hand a warm feeling comes over Jack, even Mother Christmas has to take a pause and look at him. Releasing her grip she says, "Young man, just plant yourself wherever you like, I'll bring you a bite to eat."

Looking back at the startled lady, Jack smiles, "could you give me a few I have a couple of friends joining me soon."

With a curious stare, "Of course, just let me know when you're ready"

Jack watches as the gray haired woman goes from table to table, serving those who are left, and bringing nothing but cheer to their faces. A half hour passes and Jack begins to worry about his blind friend. Just as he's about to get up and go look for him, the door opens and a man in uniform enters and starts looking about the place. He looks like he is in his early thirties, and a bit out of place here. Raising his hand Jack waves him over, "are you Mr. Connors? "

The man in uniform walks over, "well it's Captain Connors, U.S. Army Air Corp., are you the man that called?"

Jack motions for the young Captain to sit down, "Yeah that would be me. I guess your old friend and my new friend is running a tad late."

Sitting down the man in uniform smiles, "yeah he's been like that for years."

Mother Christmas again rushes over and introduces herself to the new guest and again Jack, and now also Captain Connors get a warm feeling.

Jack and the Captain make a bit of small talk, but both seemed to be transfixed by the gray haired hostess cheering up all those about the place. Soon it starts to get dark outside and the place begins to empty. Jack looks at the Captain who too looks a bit inpatient. "Tell me Captain, is he always this late?"

Smiling back at Jack, "Yep, he was even late the first time I met him a dozen or so years back."

The place is now empty with the exception of Jack, Captain Connors, and the cheerful Miss Walker. The old gray haired hostess walks over and sits down, "What a day! I've been doing this since I was a young woman, but I tell ya, the mileage is adding up. I have enough stew left for maybe four more; you two want a bite yet?"

Jack and Captain Connors both decide it's time to eat; their friend can finish the rest of the pot. Connors looks at his watch, "Well I have been officially off duty for a few minutes, time to loosen this outfit up a bit."

Laughing Jack can tell the young man's discomfort, "What you're not used to the uniform yet?"

Connors and Jack begin to talk and Jack finds out that Connor also had lost everything in the stock market crash, but because of his experience, was given the rank of Captain when he joined the Army Air Corp.

More time has passed as Mother Christmas finishes cleaning the dishes and takes a seat with the two men. Connor unbuttons his shirt a bit and pulls out a trinket from around his neck, "I don't know if I will ever get used to tucking this in"

Jacks eyes widen up as he looks at the Airman, "Where did you get that?"

Lifting up the two silver objects, "Oh, these? There called Dog Tags, two of them so you can be identified if you get killed or blown up. Too many men that were killed were never identified in the Great War."

Jacks fingers begin to shake as he points, "No, no ...not those... that other one."

"Oh, that, that's my good luck charm. I've had it since I can remember. I think it's a family heirloom or something."

Looking at the man before him Jack's face goes blank, "What is your full name Captain?"

With a puzzled look on his face, the Captain answers, "J.P. or John Paul Connors. My mother said I had a different last name at birth but I took my stepdads name."

As Jack stares at the man before him Miss Walker too gets a bewildered look on her face.

Jack clears his throat, "Well, J.P. or John Paul, my real name is John Paul Parsons, and that good luck charm you have, I gave to you before your mother left me. It was given to me by my mother, who I was told died, and who was half..."

A shaky female voice interrupts, "... Lakota Indian, named Sara, who got it from her grandfather and gave it to her son, John. Who she was told died of the fever."

Three pairs of eyes begin to well up as they all realize what is happening. They all three stand and embrace as tears begin to flow.

Jacks trembling voice breaks the silence, "but how can this be? Your blind friend Helmut had me call you."

J.P. fights back the tears, "What? Helmut's not blind, but there was a blind stranger who kept us from killing each other during the Great War."

Sara walks back to the wall by the counter and pulls a picture frame off the wall, and faces it towards the on looking eyes. In unison the both scream, "That's Him!"

Sara rejoins her newfound son and grandson, "This picture was taken on Christmas Eve, 1883, almost fifty years ago."

J.P chimes in, "I met him over twelve years ago."

Finally Jack shakes his head, "But he looks the same today, when I saw him, just a few hours ago! How can that be?"

As the three stand in awe, Sara, softly whispers,
"Thank you, I now truly have all the riches I have ever desired"

Three souls are now weeping silently, drenched in tears of joy.

Breaking the silence, a sudden tapping noise and a familiar tune breaks the silence from outside. As all three rush toward the door, the long white strands pass by the window whistling a familiar tune.

Opening the door, the snowflakes from above become absorbed in their tears of joy.

Looking down the sidewalk they see nothing …

On this 'Silent Night'

Memory Lane

A slight dusting of snow begins to accumulate on the once green fertile lawns on the afternoon of Christmas Eve. A pair of old eyes, with their own silver dusting on top, think back to this past, long year. It has been a tough one for Hank as his mind thinks back to more pleasant times. Walking to the kitchen, Hank grabs a cookie, pours what's left of the morning's coffee into a cup, and places it in the microwave.

Taking a bite of the store bought cookie, his taste buds sure miss what once was, not that long ago. Grabbing his coffee, Hank sits in the silent living room, looking out the window, watching the feathery, heavenly whites gently floating to the ground. The couch, once happily occupied by the love of his life, Lilly, now sits empty. The house across the street once filled with his and Lilly's best friends, Al and Trudy, has been torn apart and remodeled to the liking of the new young owners, removing most of what time had left on the old place and Hank's memories. The old clock chimes three o'clock, and tells Hank he's got to get a move on ...; he's been invited to Christmas Eve dinner.

This Christmas Eve, Father John had invited Hank to join him, and all of those who were preparing for midnight Mass to a special dinner. Offering to pick Hank up, the old veteran declined, because he wanted to walk the six blocks to the church.

Walking into the bedroom and opening the closet, Hank takes out his Christmas suit, as Lilly used to call it. Turning toward the bed, Hank reflects on that fateful day in January of this past year. Waking up early, Hank had decided to let Lilly sleep as he wanted to surprise her, by making her favorite breakfast. Coming back with a tray, like a fancy butler, Hank spoke the words, "Good morning my Beautiful Sunshine, time for breakfast!"

But there was no happy smile, and those surprised, beautiful eyes looking back at him.

The motionless Lilly, told Hank, their breakfasts would be no more.

Now with his suit on, Hank grabs a pair of gripping sole shoes Lilly had bought him and puts them on, ready to leave for the church. Securing his coat and hat, Hank takes a look at the old house that was once filled with everything he loved.

Having bought the house in 1947, right after he and Lilly were married; the then twenty year old couple lived there for seventy four years. Soon Hank would have to part with it … not because the ninety five year old body was bad, but the cost of taxes and utilities took both his, and Lilly's retirement income, to maintain the old place. Come the next year, Hank would have to sell it, alomg with all the memories.

Opening the front door, a boy is standing across the street at Al and Trudy's old place, smiling and waving hello to Hank. Never having seen the kid before, Hank gives a smile and a wave as he begins his slow walk down the street.

Soon Hank stops to take a look at the hill rising up across the end of the street. Once a bare flowered area with a stream running through; it is now covered with high-end condos, and the stream now runs below the street, through concrete piping. Hank gets a smile as this is where he and Al, Lilly and Trudy had all met so long ago. It was during that time, in the 1930's, when the Great Depression was making life hard and money was scarce. But when the young couples met by the hill and stream, it was all fun and games. Al had come running down from upstream because some other boys wished to do him harm, as "black kids need to stay with their own". As the three boys started beating Albert up, Hank jumped in to help the scrappy black kid. Soon they sent the three other boys running, and Albert and Hank shook hands deciding that whoever wanted to play on this hill can … no matter what their color. Soon two little girls, one black, one white, named Trudy and Lilly, who also had a secret friendship, would now also openly play together, without bullies from both sides saying that they can't.
Hank smiles broadly as he softly says, "We were the Little Rascals."

Walking another half block, the corner liquor store comes into view. Hank shakes his head, "Well old Mrs. O'Malley would surley be having a fit. That store filled with intoxicating spirts, has probably become haunted by the ole Mrs..."
It had once been, "O'Malley's Market", where Mrs. O'Malley ran things her way. Her old husband had been a diligent consumer of the spirits and had driven his car off the road and killed himself. Thus the widow O'Malley was a prohibitionist and forbid anyone working for her to ever smell like liquor.

It was there that both Hank and Al got jobs, mainly because her son Dan, was a tad bit on the lazy side, and he would sneak off with women to have a drink, … or two. Hank told Dan that he and Al would do all the deliveries and clean up for him. Dan agreed to pay Hank ten cents an hour, but Al would only get five cents, "Because he was colored". Hank agreed, but unknown to both Dan and Al, would give Al twenty cents a day from his pay. Hank figured they both worked the same, so they should both make sixty cents a day. "Man did Al and I impress Trudy and Lilly when we took them to the movie theater."

Taking off his hat to scratch his head, Hank again sees the boy from earlier smiling at him from the backseat of a slow moving car.

Hank can now see the church steeples. They are also getting a dusting of snow in the distance; he's now about half way there. Flying above the steeples, planes are coming in for landings at the distant airport. They appear to float by like angels. Back in the early days of prop planes, the now high school and football stadium was the airstrip. That is where both Hank and Al got their first experience with flying from Hank's wild Uncle Bob. Bob was a crop duster in the early years. Later on Uncle Bob would give flying lessons to help pay the bills. Hank asked his crazy uncle if he would be willing to give him and Al flying lessons, and how much it would cost. Now ole Uncle Bob would take off his cowboy hat and think. "Man, if I would be seen giving a colored boy flying lessons that would ruffle some feathers in this town. Perfect, I'm that fox in the hen house anyway."

Uncle Bob made an agreement with the boys, they would pay for the fuel and help him with upkeep and repairs, and he'll have the boys flying in no time. Both Hank and Al learned to fly and repair airplane engines along with the other major flying components. Something the two boys would someday find was more beneficial than they ever realized at the time. Uncle Bob was a mentor, and a practical joker. He even would pay for their flying lesson fuel, if they would just find that ole cowboy hat … that periodically would fly off while dusting a field. Those same fields that used to sprout the annual harvest now have the permanent growth of dwellings upon them.

With the wintertime sun ready to bid an early farewell, the lights of the season start to come aglow as Hank makes his slow memorable way towards the church.
Looking across the street, Hank has to laugh at the retro 50's style diner. The new neon signs seem to blend in with the Christmas decor, but it was never one of those places …
it used to be Papa Pizzino's Pizza. One of the first pizza places outside of the big eastern cities. Papa Pizzino and his wife, who they all called, Mama Diane, would run the place for fifty years. It was the place, that he and Al took Lilly and Trudy on their first real dinner date, back in the summer   of 1941.

Papa Pizzino, a big burly man with a signature handlebar moustache, was always cheerful. He would play loud Italian music, which he would always sing to. Not a bad voice either. The only time ole Papa showed any sign of anger, was when the four teenagers were on their first of many dinner dates there.

Having seated the four at a nice table up front, one of the city council members came in with his date. Getting ready to seat the councilman at a table across from the teenagers, the man objected.

"I'm sorry this won't do. Could you re-seat those young people with their colored company to a back table first?"

Well, ole Papa Pizzino just got a big smile on his face and looked the man in the eyes, "Oh, so you wanta me to mova dem cause two of dem are a different color?"

The councilman smiled back, "Yes, that would be great, you know black folks shouldn't be in pizza places, up front you know."

Papa Pizzino put his big paw on the man's shoulder, "Yes a, I knowa, I knowa you. You dat same a man nota so long ago dat was marching upa the street with a white a robe saying, 'We don'ta want any black people, Jewish, Mexican, Chinese, Irish, or Italian Catholics ruining the town'. Yes I remember you, an now I tella you nicely, geta out and a never come a back. You is a no longer welcome here."

No sooner had Papa said that, when Mamma Diane had the door open with a quick, "arrivederci".

Pizzino Pizza would stay open until 1985 when Mamma and Papa retired to the warm shores of Florida for the rest of their years, but not before Hank, Al, Lilly and Trudy would spend many of those years at their favorite dinner place.

Now seeing the church lights come on as the dark shadows of winter move in, a single beam of the last of the day's sun, tells Hank, the dusting of snow is probably over.

Taking one last look over at the former Pizzino's place, Hank sees that boy again, inside the now retro diner at the window in a booth waving at him. Thinking, "Huh, his parents must be the owners, probably just cleaning up."
Giving the boy a smile and a slight tip of the hat and a quick wave back, Hank is almost there to the church, just one last building to pass on this block. It's now the town library, but back in Hank's day, it was his high school. A place a certain teacher named Mr. Quint, set both he and Al straight on learning and not goofing around.

During that time, the black kids were required to sit in the back of the classrooms in most cases. But, Mr. Quint was the exception to those stupid rules. He did not care where anyone sat, and would discipline any student who had any problem with it. All who thirsted for knowledge could sit wherever they wished. Besides being a teacher, Mr. Quint was also the school's baseball coach. He had seen both Hank, and especially Al play baseball during the summer at the old sandlot. Al had a swing like he had rarely seen in all his years of coaching. If he were white, he would surley go to the majors someday. But even now, this kid would make a rooster in the Negro Leagues. Hank had a mean pitch. His fastball was one of the fastest Quint had ever seen in a fifteen year old. It seemed that no matter what teams came up against Hank and Al, the two were always on the winning side. But, both boys had only one thing in mind after school, and that was heading to the airstrip and planes. So much so, their school work began to take a nose dive.

That is when Mr. Quint told the two to stay after class one life changing day. Knowing both boys were smarter than their grades showed, it was just their vision of learning that needed a bit clearing up. He knew that the boys were working on becoming pilots, so Quint put a map with numbers and all kinds of calculations in front of them.

"So you two are flying from here to Littleton, you have this many pounds of mail to deliver, along with this much other cargo. Your airplane gets this many miles out of a tank of fuel when there's no cargo. How many miles do you get with the cargo, and a headwind of twenty miles an hour? Do you have enough fuel to make it to Littleton?"

Both Al and Hank look at their teacher like deer in the headlights. They both have no clue. Neither boy had thought of this. Al finally speaks up, "Mr. Quint, you obviously know Hank and I are very passionate about flying. We are both going to solo pretty soon. I know you mean well but…"

Quint cuts Al off, "I don't mean well, I just want you two flying knuckleheads to realize, just because you know how to fly an airplane, and rebuild an airplane … you need more to stay alive in an airplane. I fear that soon the United States will get drawn into this war that is destroying Europe. Soon, you two might be in the skies fighting to survive. The more knowledge you have to go with your skills, the better chances you are going to have to survive what I fear is coming."

Hank looks at Mr. Quint, "So what made you want to learn and be so smart?"

Quint smiles at the two, "I had to. There was no choice other than to live the way my family has lived for many generations … as farm hands. You see I have a secret. I know I can trust you two. I was once known as, Mr. Quintana. That's right. I'm a lighter shade than the average Mexican, and in order to get a better job, I had to learn as much, and as best as I could. And with the way times were, I changed my name. It's the only thing I regret."

Both Al and Hank look at each other and understand. And both from that day forward would study and be Mr. Quint's best students the rest of the year.
On December 7th of that year, what their favorite teacher had foretold, came true, America entered World War Two.

Hank would take a few more steps then again stop and look across the street at the new cell phone store. It's the same old building that was the recruiting office after the attack on Pearl Harbor by the Japanese. It still stands tall all these years later. Hank remembers how he and Al wanted to enlist at fifteen, as they already knew how to fly and were ready to fight. The recruiter laughed a bit, but was also honest with Al. "There's no chance that you and your best friend will be flying together, … with him being colored, but, … when you get close to the age, I did hear of a pilot training camp just for negro's in a place called, Tuskegee Alabama."
Both boys talked with Uncle Bob, before he left to be a training pilot for the Army Air Corp. Both boys studied hard in school, worked as much as they could and spent the rest of their time with Lilly and Trudy.

The two also did something unexpected; they cheated on their birth certificates, and enlisted at seventeen in 1943.
Al would be granted a spot in Tuskegee, thanks to Uncle Bob, who knew the base commander.

Hank shakes his head and laughs out loud, "that ole sweet son of a bitch Uncle Bob was the one who told us and showed us how to fake our birth certificates."
But Uncle Bob also knew, these two boys could fly.

Al would soon become a fighter pilot, and escort the B-17's over the skies of Europe, as far as their fuel tanks would allow. The white B-17 pilots were always relieved at the sight of these Tuskegee pilots taking on enemy German fighters. Fate was also involved, as the pilot of a B-17 looked over and saw his best friend giving him the thumbs up with a big smile. That would also be Hank and Al's last mission together as once the fighter escorts had to turn back, Hank's plane was shot down and he would spend the rest of the war in a German P.O.W. camp. The old lips softly whisper into the frosty momentarily steamed air, "oh those were glorious days."

Waiting on the light to change, the old eyes see the Baptist church up on the hill decorated in lights. Hanks mind again wanders to a special place, 1946, and a special two days of weddings for two veterans. Hank and Lilly would first raise a few eyebrows at the Baptist ceremony, being the best man and matron of honor. Then the next day, Al and Trudy would do the same at the Catholic Church. It had been a learning experience for both congregations, as they now saw that skin color didn't matter to these best friends, or in the eyes of God.

Crossing the street, Hank's eyes become saddened as he took a deep breath. The cemetery had now come into view along with the large old cottonwood tree. Just to the right of this majestic old tree, lie the final resting places of his Lilly and their only son, Henry. Soon after the marriage, both Al and Hank would become, "expectant fathers", as they would say. Henry would also have a best friend, James, the son of Al and Trudy. Hank and Lilly could not have any more children, but Al and Trudy had eight in total, James being the oldest. Hank went to work for Boeing, while Al stayed in the military and flew the newest jets and trained pilots for thirty years before retiring and moving in across the street from his best friends'. Just like Hank and Al, Henry and James were as one, and tackled some of the same color differences as their parents had. Both had enlisted, and become Green Berets. They went on many missions in Vietnam together. Both were on their way back from a certain mission, and would soon be sent home. But their helicopter was shot down, killing them both. It was a somber day when the caskets came home with their two heroes inside, and the whole town mourned along with both sets of parents. A cold tear runs down the wrinkled old face and is softly wiped away with a warming coat sleeve. "I love you two so much".

Reaching the steps of the church, Father John is there to greet Hank, "You know you old stubborn fart, I would have come to get you. It must have been a miserable walk for you." Hank smiles, "goes to show how wrong you are, it was a marvelous walk through something called Memory Lane, you former little hoodlum you."

Father John walks down, gives Hank a hug, and offers to help him up the stairs, "Thanks, but no thanks Padre, I walked all the way here as I have done for so many years, these last few steps up, well, they too mean something. Besides I still remember a smiling choir boy, offering to help me up the stairs after I broke my ankle, then he stole my wallet."

Now Father John has to start laughing, "Oh boy, yeah, I was hoping all these years later, you would have forgotten about that."
Hank smiles and gives the priest a wink, "not likely".

Hank was right … back in the day, Father John was a hoodlum. Back then he went by Thomas John, and the priest of the church at that time, Father Steven, had his hands full. Thomas was into everything that raised eyebrows and caused concern. The young hoodlum was caught numerous times shoplifting, ditching school to go fishing, and even stole Sheriff Nick's patrol car and took a bunch of teenagers for a joy ride, with the lights flashing and sirens blaring. And all of this happened before Thomas was fifteen. Then came the day that Thomas hooked up with some older boys and they stole a bunch of beer from the liquor store. With ten cases of beer in the trunk and more being consumed by five mouths in the newly stolen Monte Carlo, the alcohol made the underage consumers feel invincible. The five felt that way all the way up to the point of trying to beat the coal train to the railroad crossing. Thomas was in the back passenger side, looking out the window when the cheering and yelling came to an abrupt stop and the air was filled with the sounds of breaking glass and crunching metal.

When Thomas opened his eyes, only he was left sitting upon a torn seat nestled within some shrubbery alongside the railroad tracks. The stunned boy and seat were about the only things left of the new car. Still dazed and a bit woozy, the cut on his forehead made Thomas's injuries look far worse than they really were.

Thomas could hear the sirens in the distance, when a man walked up to him, long coat, suit and tie, hat like an old school detective, "Hey, Thomas, you're the lucky one tonight, make the best of it. You were given another chance."
The figured slowly turned and walked off as emergency vehicles arrive.
A medic rushes over to Thomas, 'Hey kid, let me take a look at that, you hurting anywhere else?"
Thomas shakes his head, "no", as a police officer approaches, "Son, I hope you can tell me what happened here tonight, as you are the only one who ever can."
Thomas was in a state of shock as he watched white blankets being draped over the parts of his former friends, "I'm not hurting, but why didn't that old detective guy help? He just turned and walked off. The guy didn't even check to see if he could do something for the other guys."
The police officer looks at Thomas, "Son, I was the first one here on the scene along with the medics, what guy are you talking abou?"
Thomas went on to describe the man in great detail as the officers face begins to drop. Thomas had just described Detective Hudson, a longtime member of the police force, who had died of a heart attack earlier that day.
Thus the hoodlum days were over and Thomas would go on to follow in the footsteps of Father Steven.

Father John now holds the heavy door open for Hank, who walks in feeling like he's entering a place for the first time … even though he and Lilly had been coming here for over seventy years. But on this Christmas Eve's Midnight Mass, he would be sitting alone at their spot in the seventh row.

Looking at the caring eyes of the former hoodlum, "If you don't mind, I'd like to sit at our spot before we eat dinner."

With a soft hand on Hank's back, the caring priest understands, "No problem Hank, I think dinner is in about a half an hour away. Some of the members are here to do last minute decorating and go over some of tonight's program. Some even brought their kids; it's going to be a long night." Both faces smile in agreement. As Hank slowly walks to his and Lilly's spot while Father John heads back to the dining room.

Hank sits down and gets the feeling that the love of his life is sitting beside him. Looking at the front of the church, Hank starts to think about how many times he sat here, and many times had to occupy his mind with something else, to not fall asleep during some of Father Steven's long sermons. Hank remembers when Henry was baptized and Al and Trudy were the Godparents. Hank laughs, "Well, we sure raised a few eyebrows that day didn't we." Hank used to tell Al and Trudy, "Us Catholics sit, kneel, stand on Sunday's, I think it's to keep us awake. Now you Baptist's, at least you get a high energy show for your donation."

Looking at the crucifix, Hank can almost make out every detail in the carving by memory, having looked at it for so many years. Just about to look away … there he is again… that same little boy waving at him from behind a pew in the first row. Hank again smiles and waves back, thinking, as the boy runs off, "His parents are going to have one very tired kid after Midnight Mass." Hearing a few other children's laughter and voices, Hank feels a bit of the old Christmas Spirit, even though it seems, he is the last of his time.

Closing his eyes momentarily, Hank is in a place his heart will never forget. Just as he's dreaming about a once so special time in his life, a sudden movement next to him brings him back to the present. Looking down, Hank sees a little girl, no older than six looking up at him with her hazel eyes, "I'm Sabrina, and you were snoring like a seal, Father John wanted me to come get you to eat dinner, and you have to eat all of it or no dessert, that's the rules."

Seeing the innocent little eyes in her festive red Christmas dress, Hank gets a big smile as this little girl is the first one who has sat that close since Lilly. Standing up, he reaches out his hand, "Okay Sabrina, you show me where we need to go. And I hope they have my favorite raw fish dinner waiting."

The little eyes get a bit confused, "raw fish? That's gross! Why would you want raw fish?"

Giving the Christmas Belle a wink, "but that's what seals eat, isn't it?" The touch of the little hand leading him to the dining area gives Hank warmth like he has not felt in some time. He again thinks, "Now this is becoming a Christmas Mass I will never forget."

Being that he is the eldest at dinner, Father John had arranged for Hank to be seated at the head of the table, and out of nowhere, Sabrina asked if she could sit beside him, if that is, there aren't any raw fish. Father John even turned over the Christmas Eve dinner prayer to Hank.

Standing up, tall and straight, Hank closes his eyes, "Lord, I know this has been the toughest year of my life, but I am still so very grateful to be here tonight surrounded by so many full of love on this blessed night. I thank you for all the years, and for all of the people I have had the great pleasure to share those years with. I thank you for this great meal that we are about to receive … in Jesus' name, Amen. Oh and P.S., maybe next year we can have some raw fish, right Sabrina?"

Now the little eyes get big and a smile goes with them, "Right Mr. Seal."
Some at the table have no clue of what just went on, but it matters not to an old man and those young smiling eyes.

Looking around the festive dinner table Hank can see people of many ages, all of them younger than he. Seeing his dinner date is done with her food, the special Christmas Eve creampuff was next on Sabrina's list.

Watching and listening, Hank looks around and then it hits him, "Where's that smiling and waving young boy I have seen all afternoon?" Indulging in his after dinner dessert of a chocolate brownie, the only thing Hank can think is, "That little guy is probably crashed out somewhere."

Father John opens up the study room, filled with Christmas movies ready for the youngsters to watch while the adults have a toast of wine, and prepare for the Midnight Mass festivities, which will begin in about four hours. Hank is asked if he wants to come watch movies with his little date, and takes Sabrina up on the offer. The old soul is feeling very young and blessed again, thanks to this little girl. It is a special memory that is being absorbed both in Hank's mind and heart, as well as the big heart of a little Christmas Belle.

Some of the children snooze for a while, but not little Sabrina. She went to get popcorn balls for herself and Hank, along with some wet wipes, "so their clothes don't get sticky".

It was not too much longer that the Church began to fill with parishioners. Hank too made his way out, and Sabrina asked her parents if she could sit with Hank, which was of course granted. Other parishioners, who had known Hank and Lilly for years, had to smile and got a warm feeling as they saw that Hank did not have to sit alone on this so special of nights. From the first song to the sermon and the last song of, "Silent Night", the midnight Mass was as special as it could be. And when a little hand grabbed and held on to Hank's older weathered hand, for an old soul, that was just the best topping for a night he never expected to be this way. A little smiling, waving boy had started it off, and a little Christmas Angel had ended the night. With the service over, Sabrina gave Hank a big hug; "Merry Christmas Mr. Seal"

Hank could do nothing but glow, "Merry Christmas Sabrina, you gave me the best present ever."

Hank stayed seated as the now exhausted people said their goodbyes and Merry Christmas's to Hank. Father John had just a few things left to do then he would give Hank a ride home.

Before he could disappear, Hank waved the former bad boy over, "Hey, my favorite hoodlum, I want to give you this." Handing Father John a letter, the tired priest started reading, then looked a Hank, "Hank are you sure? Is this what you want? I mean I don't know what to say…"

Hank interrupts, "Say nothing. I know Lilly would feel the same way. Now go get your stuff done, these old eyes are getting a bit heavy."

Father John gives Hank a hug, "Merry Christmas to you, my favorite old fart." Hank again sits and starts to reflect on the memories made that night and how so special it was. Shutting his eyes for a second, Hank is again on a wonderful journey.

A sudden noise awakens Hank as a smiling face waves at him from a few rows back. Seeing no one else around, Hank begins to worry, "Oh my …just like in that Christmas movie, they forgot the kid."

Standing up Hank walks back to the boy who stands waiting for him. Reaching out his little hand, the little boy motions Hank towards the door.

Hank looks at him, "So you think your family is still out there?" The boy nods his head in agreement and starts to lead Hank.

"Alright young whipper snapper, let's go see if we can find them. Now, if we don't, we'll come right back in here and Father John will probably know who you belong to, okay?" Again the young head nods in agreement. Walking toward the doors, holding the young hand, the heavy doors seem to slowly blow themselves open.

Walking out, Hank cannot believe his eyes. At the bottom of the steps are those he once knew. Papa and Mamma Pizzino, Uncle Bob, Mr. Quint, Al, Trudy, Henry, James and walking up toward him, Lilly. Thinking he is surely dreaming, Hank looks over at the young boy that is holding his hand, and can see, it is no longer a young boy, but a man with the most heavenly peaceful glow that he has ever see.

With a voice that fills the ears with enchantment, the words softly flow out, "You are home Hank, no one will ever leave you again." Hank slowly walks down to Lilly's awaiting arms, followed by Al and Trudy along with all the loving rest.

Father John looks over at Hank, "Okay old fart, let's go." Waiting a few seconds, the tired priest walks over toward the sitting figure. Father John's smile fades within a few feet of Hank. Looking at the still face with the peaceful smile upon it, Father John makes the sign of the cross,
"Merry Christmas you old fart, now you are forever with all those you have missed so."

A young girl is saddened to find out that her, "Mr. Seal", has gone to Heaven. The young figure would sit in row seven, on the isle, for decades to come, and will someday also travel along that very special road known as, **"Memory Lane"**.

Credo

(I Believe)
Part 3 of 'The Trilogy'

The brief warmth of the days last light would generate a big smile on so many on this day. Instead he feels as cold on the inside as the snow feels beneath his feet. He was chosen, and he has served. He has not wanted to die, until now. As the wind briefly ruffles his long white hair, a tear gently flows down his cheek. He sheds it not for himself, but for those that have forgotten.

This December 24th 2050, is the same as it has been for the past 20 years. It was empty of all meaning … even for those who once believed in the good of man. Thinking back to 20 years ago, he remembers as if it only happened yesterday. The World Council had banned all religions. It had come to a point, where humans only believed in humans. Those who resisted were sent off, never to return. Christmas was no more, and the goodwill to our fellow man was replaced by the goodwill of the World Council.

He had made his way to this place of solitude, fearing that anyone he would help, as he had done thousands of times in the past, would be sent away. The World Council knew where he was, and he knew they knew. For twenty years he had been hoping to once again bestow a miracle on this Holiest of Nights. But this Christmas Eve was once again like the dead leaves that blow in the wind… memories of yesterday, with no guarantees of tomorrow.

As he whistles softly, a small chipmunk climbs up a wooden barrel beside the old wooden bench that he sits upon. Reaching into his pocket, he pulls out a small piece of bread. Gently laying his hand on the barrel, he feels the tender little feet step into his hand and enjoy the morsel before it.

"Merry Christmas to you, my little friend … you are the only friend I have had in years." Then looking towards the heavens he whispers, "Lord, I have failed you. Surely I have given mankind so many blessings on this day of your birth, but now, does man still need God? Does God still need me? I will continue to serve you as I have promised so many years ago… but if a shepherd has no flock, and only wolves exist, Dear Lord, who am I to save?"
Feeling the little chipmunk nibble away at the bread, his heart feels empty. It's an emptiness that he has not felt in a long, long, time.

A slight wind blows his hair aside as a sudden "Crack" echoes from the distance. Startled the man's little friend grabs the remaining piece of bread and takes off.

Soon footsteps can be heard making their way through the frozen snow coming toward him. As they stop, his blind eyes cannot see, but his ears tell him of the beasts that are not far from him, beasts he once knew so well. A few seconds later another sound in the snow … more footsteps making their way towards him. In his blindness, he knows that these footsteps are from a more dangerous beast, as they are human footsteps.

Stopping not ten yards before him, a voice breaks the silence, "It's you, I didn't know you were truly real, until now."

Sitting up straight, being at a disadvantage, he lightly moves his long white hair behind him, "Well, to say I am surprised is an understatement. May I ask who I have the pleasure of speaking with? Also how have you found me? And why is a young lady so far away from civilization on what was once, Christmas Eve?"

Taking a few steps forward the woman clears her throat, "Well, a picture told me about you; it is a picture of you, this cabin, this bench, and this barrel. The only thing missing is your hand across the barrel with a small piece of bread in it and a fat little chipmunk eating."

The perplexed ancient one brings his hand up to his chin, "A picture you say? Who would take a photo of me way out here?"

Reaching into her pocket the woman takes out a piece of paper, "Well it's not a photo, but a drawing, by a ten year old girl. Somehow she knew, you would be here, right at this moment."

With a long forgotten smile, he speaks softly,
"So, where is this ten year old girl? And where does she live?
But most puzzling … why have you come here because of a
ten year olds drawing?"

The woman approaches closer and touches the man's
hand, "Because that little ten year old girl who drew this
picture, stands before you, right now."

Scratching his head, "Now, young lady? I may be blind,
but I am not deaf. Your voice is that of a young woman, not of
a ten year old child"

The young woman kneels before him, "This picture, along
with some numbers and this date, I drew on December 24,
2029. Twenty one years ago, on my birthday, after the most
beautiful lady I have ever seen, woke me, and somehow
showed me what to draw."

Placing his hand upon the kneeling woman's head …
"Child, I too once saw this lady. I now think I know, what is
before us."

The woman looks into her reflection in the blind man's
glasses and softly speaks the words, "Ana ba'yah mishal b-
shlamak̲".

The stunned old face once again smiles, "Now there's a
language I have not heard in more years than I can
remember. Young lady, your Aramaic is even proper, asking
me how I am doing." Then he responds, "Eímai kalá"

The woman smiles back and replies, "Your Greek is is up to par as well. I am glad you are fine."

Standing up as the last of the days light disappears over the mountains, "Come, let's go inside as the coldness of the night will soon be upon us young lady"

Standing, the woman touches the man's hand, "There's no time for that. Can you ride a horse? We need to make it to a cave a few miles away before total darkness comes. We will then have maybe one hour before they find us. I'll explain along the way"

Walking a few steps to the cabin door, the old hands grab a hat, a coat, and a long bag. With a John Wayne voice he smiles, "Head em up, move em out. Let's ride"

The young lady leads the blind stranger toward the horses. Looking up, she sees a star in the horizon making its way upward into the sky. Thinking to herself, "Even though it is just twilight, that star seems brighter than it should be."

The blind man abruptly stops just short of the horses, "I am mystified. By now I should somehow know the name of the person I have met … yet this time, I have, nothing. What is your name?"

Looking back at the mirrored glasses, "Star, my name is Star. Now what is your name, and I mean your real name, given to you at birth or when you were young."

Adjusting his hat the man realizes that he has dodged this question many many times, yet this time, he feels compelled to answer. "Ambrosios, my given name is, Ambrosios."

With a smirk on her face she responds, "Ambrosios. That's Greek for immortal. What a fitting name." Pulling on the man's hand, "Now come on, time is not on our side."

Reaching the horses, Ambrosios gently strokes the nose of the horse before him, "Hello Diamond, what a beautiful girl you are. Come, let's go on a journey."

As the horse nudges the blind man toward the saddle, Star is a bit surprised, "How did you know the horse was a female, and how did you know her name is Diamond?"

Adjusting his hat as he saddles up, "It's what I have done … No, it's what I do!" Kicking the horse lightly, Diamond and her blind occupant take off in the direction of Star's shelter. Star quickly saddles up and takes the lead to the mysterious cave. The night begins to move in, yet the sky is becoming brighter as the rising star's reflection upon the earth widens.

With his bag secure, the twilight ride brings back a few memories to the sightless rider … memories that he has always treasured. After a few minutes he asks, "Star, why are we going to a cave on this cold, crisp Christmas Eve night? I'm usually the one to take someone on a journey on this blessed night. That is until now."

Star looks back at the blind man who appears at home on a horse, "Ambrosios, I'll tell you everything. Everything I have been working on for so long, once we get inside the cave. Until then, well, let's just get there as quickly as possible."

The two pick up the pace as they make their way through the starlit snow covered hills, toward the opening of a secluded cave. Stopping in front of it, Ambrosios raises an eyebrow, "Star, how did you know that this cave was here?"

Getting off her horse, Star gives her companion a wink, "I didn't until now. It's just what 'I' do".

The infamous smile appears beneath the dark glasses, "Touché".

Getting off his horse the blind rider realizes he has left his cane back at the cabin, "Well then, guess I gotta give this new 21st century contraption a try" Reaching into his pocket he pulls out a slim cylinder and pushes a button. The once six inch object telescopes into a cane, just his size.
Star, amused, just watches as the tapping man walks by her, "Meet ya inside, cause, baby it's cold outside."

Star smiles as she watches him disappear into the cave. Taking off the saddles and placing them inside the cave, Star then brings her bags inside. Reaching into her pocket she pulls out a round object, and sets it down. Within seconds it illuminates the cave, and she can see her surroundings, "There we go, that lights up the place beautifully."

Pushing the button to retract his cane, "Thanks, don't need this no more, love what you have done to the place." A big smile appears on an old blind face.

Star looks at the smiling man before her, "You always been this big of a wise cracker?"

Ambrosios gets a serious look on his face, "Did you just call me a cracker?"

A few seconds pass as the laughter echo throughout the cave. Star reaches into her saddlebag and pulls out another small box and pushes a button, "There we go, this should heat up this place in no time, yet it won't give out any infrared heat signals, give me a few minutes to set up my other equipment, then I'll explain everything. I have worked toward this moment, since I first drew that picture, twenty one years ago on this very night. Here's some beef jerky to enjoy. I know it's now illegal, but that's why I enjoy it."

Tossing the bag in Ambrosios direction, the blind man's hands snatch it out of midflight, "Thank you Star. Illegal jerky? I wonder what my old friend Red Cloud would have thought of that."

Star begins to set up her equipment, stopping briefly to snatch a piece of jerky from a smiling blind man's hands. After about fifteen minutes of rushing around, she sits down next to her companion, smiles, and grabs the last of the jerky from his fingertips.

Adjusting his glasses as if he was getting ready to read something he says, "Star, why have you come to me? You know if they catch you, or if they find out that you came to see me, the World Council will punish you severely. Child, if you only knew what these eyes have seen. Man has turned on his fellow man time and time again. This time I fear, because man was given free will, he will go down a path of no return. I have always wished for two things on this blessed of nights, I feel that both may never come to pass."

Star sits up, "Maybe, just maybe, you and I can change something on this night … something we both have been blessed to have been touched by. I will go first, and tell you my tale. I have studied you. I don't know *what* you are but I know *why* you are." Standing up Star reaches into her bag and pulls out a small bottle of wine, and two collapsible cups. "I'll open this, and then we can start. Once I do, this may be the last chance of ever hearing the words, '*Merry Christmas*' again."

Pouring two glasses of wine, Star takes a sip, "I'll go first as I have to ask you to do something after I am done that may give us both hope".

Clanking his plastic cup to hers, "May God give us strength, and I give you what you need."

Star looks at the reflection of herself in the glasses of the man she has studied since she was told, "he's real".
Taking another sip, Star begins. "I was born on December 24, 2019 to a light brown haired Spanish woman who was born in Madrid named, Sophia. She met my father at a Christmas Eve service where he was playing guitar, his name was..."

Ambrosios interrupts, "Jamal, yes now it's coming to me child. Jamal, is the city boy who once upon a time made an everlasting promise to his mother. Now this is becoming clearer. In the past I could pick things up sooner. Sorry, I now know of your birth and why you are here, but go on with your story, that is something I don't know."

Seeing that his smile is now gone, Star continues, "Daddy would always say a man came out of nowhere, saved his life, and disappeared. He referred to him as a Christmas angel. When I drew that picture of you and all the numbers, the next day, I showed it to my daddy. He cried and tenderly touched your image. It's as if he knew that the next year the World Council would banish all religion and religious holidays, replacing them with their own. He told me no matter what; never show this picture to anyone. I hid it and always kept it in a safe place. Then a year later, they came for my mom, Sophia and my daddy Jamal. Daddy had warned me they would come, and trained me not to cry on the outside, even as my insides were a mess. Daddy said to be strong, for the beautiful lady that directed me to draw the picture and numbers, had a purpose for me. I cursed at my parents as they were taken away, just as my daddy instructed me to. The World Council took me away to one of their schools for special training. I learned the global satellite information systems and how to relay information to each and every household across the globe."

Taking another sip of wine Star begins to feel the pressure that has been put upon her and begins to shed tears. Sensing this emotion a blind man speaks up, "Hey, you gonna drink the rest of that wine, give me another snort, this story is getting good. Star, you and I are here at this precise moment in time, because God has made it so. Please continue.

Star pours a bit more into the two cups and continues her story, "So as a prodigy at the World Council, I had access to privileged information, and that is where you came into the picture again, and again."

"As a teenager I was allowed to go study all the artworks in the worlds' new museums, which were once houses of worship. It was at one of the earliest churches I saw an old painting, done in the 3rd century and an image caught my eye. The painting showed one of St. Peters sermons, and in the crowd, there stood a blind man with black cloth tied over his eyes, yet a smile so big. I saw the same image again in the old museums in Istanbul, once called Constantinople.
The works of Leonardo Da Vinci, Michael Angelo, and others, your face was always there. George Washington addressing the Continental Congress you again were in the crowd in that painting, but this time, you wore those dark glasses.
I know that they were made for you by Benjamin Franklin, as he referred to you in one of his early letters as: 'the most intelligent historian I have ever met, yet he was blind'."

Star continues, "History was not too hard for you, since you were there through all of it. Then when photography was born, you again appear, in Europe, The Middle East, India, Africa … you were at the Gettysburg address and at Lourdes with Bernadette and also at Fatima Portugal for the miracle of The Virgin Mary in 1917. I think that is why I am here tonight. To find out and share your story".

The smile is back on the blind face as he clears his throat, "Wow, you have been busy and have followed me along in my adventures, but I don't know how telling you everything will change anything."

Star gets up and grabs another piece of equipment from her bag and sits back down, "With this new image relator. You see if I hook this up to the side of your head, all your memories, as you tell them come alive on the screen. They now use this in the court systems as testimonials of the truth. You cannot make something up, it just projects the truth. I have been planning this night for a long time. My mother and father disappeared for this moment. What I have developed, is a way to relay the global output of your memories to all the PHS's or Personal Hologram Systems across the entire world, for everyone to view. Over the years I have planted hundreds of small rely towers in very remote places to allow satellite signals to bounce all over the world from this source. If my mathematical skills are correct, it will take the minimum of one hour for the second best programmer to break my code."

Scratching his head, "Star, you say second best, that means I am sitting next to the best. I think I know what you wish to accomplish, but when they come, and they will ...you will be in the gravest of danger. They already know my time is dependent on the Lord not them. You are a brave woman. I cannot get a feel for how this will turn out. But wait ...you say that picture that you drew had numbers, what numbers?"

Star again unfolds the picture, "At first I had no clue, but then they all made sense. A GPS guide to you and this cave, on this night, December 24, 2050. I am prepared to face whatever becomes of this, I have always had faith, and that will never change."

Drinking down his last sip, "then let us begin, for we have been chosen as many before us have been. May this blessed night give us strength."

Star now gets up and walks over to the entrance of the cave and looks out. The horses are just off to the right, as she sees the snow on the pine trees and shrubs; they have a shine to them like she has never seen before. Looking toward the sky the star above is projecting a type of light she also has never seen before.

Taking a knee she looks up, "God please give me strength when the time comes. Mom, Dad, I don't know if you can hear me, but I am here to do what has been asked of me. I am proud to be your daughter."

Getting up she walks back in to see that infamous smile, "You know Star, I think they heard you. Now let's get this time machine fired up and rock the world like it's never rocked before."

Star hooks up her wire to the side of Ambrosios's temple. She then hits a button and a hologram of the whole world pops up. Looking at the smiling man, "Okay, let's just do a quick test. Think about a memory and I'll see if it pops up on my screen.

Smiling, "Oh, let's see, I was chasing mammoths and…"

Star interrupts, "Ambrosios that's a lie! Come on, this time we'll send it out to the whole world. I'll set the clock to count down from sixty minutes. That might be all the time we have"

Taking a deep breath the smile disappears and a somber face turns to her, "I have two wishes this night, but will be satisfied with one, Star ... that God blesses you always. Begin your transmission."

The screen goes black, "Well let's see now, it was on this day, over two thousand years ago...."

Then images comes into view, it seems to be a horse stable of sorts. "Boy! Get over here and feed these horses then give them water and brush them down. I am hoping the Romans take them in exchange for my yearly taxes which are due."

An eight year boy hurries with buckets of food and starts feeding and talking to the horses, "Hello again my friends, remember me? I'm Ambrosios. Eat well, then I will give you water and brush you down. Someday you might have the privilege of being owned by the commander of the Legions himself."

As the horses seem to warm and calm to the attention of the young boy, the sound of footsteps outside draws the boys' eyes away for a moment. A man has led a woman into town on a donkey, and the couple is securing a stable down the way. Waiting for the horses to drink their fill, the boy reaches into a pocket and pulls out a small bell that his father had made for him as an infant . Moving it back and forth the simple chime brings a smile to the boy's face as he remembers back two years to his time in Greece.

His parents had both died when he was younger, and his uncle sold him to the Germanic horse trader, Boda. Whenever he rings the bell, it brings back happier days of running in fields and laughing with his mother and father. The little bell is his most prized possession. He rings it again and even the horses seem to enjoy the chimes.

Now having brushed the horses down, and secured them for the night, Boda the horse trader brings the boy some bread and dried fish. "Here you have done well little Greek. The animals look good for the sale in the morning, sleep well out here, and work well, and maybe one day, you can buy your freedom from me." The tall blond haired bearded man leaves as the boy indulges in his treat.

Night moves in, yet the sky seems to be almost as bright as day. Laying back on some straw Ambrosios notices a sudden line of individuals going by heading down the path. Getting up he looks outside and sees the brightness of the star above. He then looks down the path and sees a group of people gathering at a small stable. Camels, horses, all without their riders, and shepherds from the fields are there too. Walking down the path he slowly makes his way into the crowded stable and sees a beautiful woman holding a new born baby. He also notices men of all colors bringing gifts to this child. Walking closer, the beautiful woman smiles at him and waves him forward for a closer look. Seeing all the gifts laid about, Ambrosios reaches into his pocket and pulls out his little bell. Ringing it, the baby smiles and looks his way, without hesitation he hands the little bell to the pretty lady.

She smiles at him and nods her head. He walks out as more come to see the child, feeling no sadness for the gift he gave the baby that smiled at him that night; the boy feels warmth inside like never before.

"Forty minutes left", Star says softly as the blind man is transfixed on times long, long, ago.

The years fly by and Boda brings the now teenage boy with him on his horse roundups, "Ambrosios! Rope her and hold her! Use the tree to secure her!" Boda quickly adds another rope to the frightened kicking mare. Securing the rope Ambrosios walks slowly towards the horse, Boda yells, "Are you crazy! Let me secure this second rope, and then we can beat her into submission."

Walking toward the horse, Ambrosios talks softly, looking the horse in the eyes, Boda stops yelling and watches as the boy slowly walks up and gently pets the frightened beast. Taking off Boda's rope, he slowly walks over to the tree to untie his. Boda's eyes widen, "Boy if she runs, she will drag you, you will lose her, and I will beat you!"

Untying the rope from the tree the boy walks up to the now calm mare and walks her towards Boda, with a big smile, "She's okay now, we are friends."

This being Ambrosios first trip north to collect horses for the Romans, it seems he talks and the horses just listen to him. "Boy, you may just buy your freedom yet. Now come, you will eat with me and my family this day."

Boda, with calm horses in tow, is followed by a smiling 'horse master' as they arrive at Boda's house. A girl running out stops the teenage boy in his tracks. Her hair is that of the most golden sunshine and her eyes of the finest emeralds. His heart begins to race and his body begins to sweat.

The girl happily yells out, "Father! I am so glad you are back! Mother and I have been waiting for your arrival for days. You said last time you left, you would not leave us again. Are your words still true?" Running up and hugging her massive father, the young girl's eyes soon capture the eyes that are captivated by her beauty. Looking up at her father, "I see you have brought a guest."

Boda looks back at the apparent mesmerized boy, "What my dear Genoveea, what guest? What him? Oh my dear daughter, that's just the slave boy that I bought ten years ago. I needed his help gathering horses this year for the Romans. Guest? You are full of jokes. And yes from now on you and momma go where I go"

This is where the boy's heart should sink, but it doesn't, as two pairs of eyes looking at each other, tell it all.

"Twenty minutes left" … Smiling toward Star's direction, the once boy of so long ago nods his head.

The years have gone by and Ambrosios bought his freedom, but then his heart became enslaved by a golden haired, emerald eyed beauty, that captured him many years ago.

Living now in Jerusalem, they have a small place of their own. Boda, Genoveea's father, had retired and gone back to Germania, only to be killed by the invading Gaul's. Ambrosios still traded horses and would have to go on long trips that would break his heart until he returned to the love of his life. Inside he knew, the love he had for Genoveea was his life. Even when a man would come and preach on the hillsides to love thy neighbor, and about the Kingdom of God, his Genoveea was all that mattered, until that one day.

Coming home after a long trip, Ambrosios was alarmed to find his love not at home. Asking a few neighbors, he was even more alarmed to find out that she had been arrested for being a follower of a certain man that was crucified, named Jesus. Rushing down to the local garrison, he was more horrified to find out that she too had been crucified the day before his return. Pleading with a high ranking Roman general, that he had once sold horses to, Ambrosios was given permission to remove Genoveea's body. Whether she was alive or dead. Rushing to the site he hands the orders to the laughing guards.

Finding her not dead, but barely alive, he cuts her down and holds her tenderly in his arms as her eyes open to his face, "Oh my dear Ambrosios, I am sorry for this. I should have told you I was a follower of this man called Jesus, who they killed a month ago. He came back from the dead they say. I… I…"

Tears are rolling down the weeping man's face as he has never felt this helpless in all his life, "Genoveea, please stay with me, I will never leave you again. Please, stay"

The emerald eyes open, "I will always love you my dear, always. I will wait for you at the gates of...heaven..."

The once sparkling eyes close, and a pain like no other fills the weeping man's heart. "Oh my dear Genoveea, if this place called heaven is there, I will find you. My love for you is eternal." A broken weeping man kisses a pair of lifeless lips one last time.

In the cave, tears begin to flow and hit the rocks on the dusty floor. Star sees the once smiling man in the greatest of pain. Taking a deep breath, the heartbroken voice softly speaks, "I placed her in a tomb and wandered the streets both days and nights, as if lost in a blinding desert storm.

Sitting on a rock in front of a shop, a sudden commotion brings the grieving man back to reality. Groups of people are rushing by, entering the shop behind him. Suddenly a lady stops and looks into the heartbroken man's eyes.
He remembers her; she was the beautiful lady with the baby so many years before.

Placing her hand upon his cheek, "She is with my Son in his Kingdom now. She will always wait for you."
A man grabs her arm and helps her into the shop behind.

Within a few seconds Roman soldiers appear, and see Ambrosios sitting there, "you, have you seen a group of people fleeing this way?"

Looking up, he recognizes the garrison commander, just as the commander recognizes him. "Ambrosios, what are you doing here? Did you see anyone running this way? They are followers of this dead man Jesus. They will meet the same fate as he did. Now, did you see anyone?"

At first he wants to tell the commander, but his love prevails, "No, I did not see anyone."

The commander looks around and sees a man fleeing down a street. Sending a few soldiers in pursuit, "Are you sure you saw no one?"

Rising up, his red swollen eyes still glassed over, "I did not see a thing"

Giving Ambrosios one last look the Romans rush off. Sitting back down, a feeling comes over him as if his beloved just kissed him. A few minutes later the Romans return, and break down the door behind Ambrosios. The commander has two men apprehended along with the once trusted horse trader. Hitting Ambrosios across the face with his hand, "You lie Ambrosios, a witness told us they went in there behind you. Now they have escaped! So you didn't see anything? Secure him!" Looking at the swollen eyes before him the commander takes out his knife, "So you, a man I trusted so many times have seen nothing? Then so be it!"

Quickly the Roman blade stabs each of the swollen red eyes. Buckling in pain the solders release the blood soaked man. Looking down at the now blind man before him, "I will not kill you Ambrosios; instead I will make you suffer until you beg for death!"

"Take this lying Greek, put him on a horse, and ride him all day into the desert, then leave him and bring back the horse. Now, you'll never see anything!"

"Five minutes, then they could find us, go on quickly" again nodding his head the screen and image that are being broadcast to billions continues.

Lying out in the desert, his eyes in pain, his heart broken, a blind man wanders to and fro. Tripping over rocks, the heat beating down, and his mouth as parched as the desert sands.. Ambrosios is to the point that he wishes to just die. Falling on his face, the sands soon blow into where two eyes once were. Just as the life seems to be leaving him, a soft ringing of a distant bell brings him back to the living. The sound comes closer and closer until the touch of his hand opening, "My hand, he opened my hand and placed a small bell into it. I knew who he was, I just knew.... and then he spoke, 'Ambrosios, you once gave me your prized possession out of the goodness of a young boy's heart. It was on that night that I was born into this world. Now go forth … venture out and find the goodness in man on that same night from henceforth. I will send for you, when it is time'. Hetold me those words, over two thousand years ago."

Star looks at her hologram of the world before her, "Ambrosios! Ninety five percent of the world is watching! It's almost Christmas!"

Star seems to get a warm feeling as the screen goes blank. The blind man tips over. "Ambrosios! Are you okay? What's wrong?"

Looking in Stars direction, "I don't know ... Will all those people believe the story they have just seen as I..."
the screen comes on again as he reaches out his hand
"Star ... the small pocket in my bag ...the content inside is yours, the content within the bag, ... you'll find a use for it."
Ambrosios's voice is becoming hoarse, "Dear girl ... I told you I had two Christmas wishes. I feel that one is coming true. In all my life, I have never been so in love as I was with one. Believe..."

The infamous smile appears one last time as the screen now shows two hands being joined. As a face of a golden haired lady with emerald eyes meet a brown eyed man, with a smile of so many lifetimes.

Star opens the small pocket and pulls out a small bell. Looking over at the lifeless body, her tears cannot be controlled.

"Oh Ambrosios, I Believe, I truly Believe."

As she looks at the clock, it hits zero. The hologram being broadcast to the world, begins to have an image appear,

"I Believe"

Soon it's as if the entire world has once again come alive with "I Believe" and its being repeated billions of times.

With tears flowing, an image appears on the screen, a smiling Ambrosios, "One wish down, one to go. Merry Christmas, Star…."

As the image fades Star hears footsteps approaching. As the two figures make their way into the cave and into the light, a feeling of jubilation comes over Star,

"Mom ! Daddy! I thought you were"

All the years apart didn't matter as now they were together again. Star now knows what the other wish was, Christmas is back as the World Council concedes to the billions who voiced, "I believe." Star looks over at the bag her smiling blind friend brought and opens it. Jamal sees what's inside,

"Star, Sophia, this is the second time this has been lost and somehow it has found it's way back home… my father's old guitar."

All three walk outside as the star above shines, an old guitar comes alive and a song begins to play on this…..Silent Night…..

Merry Christmas!

Das Geschenk
(The Gift)

Jürgen war auf der Jagd. Seine Beute würde ihn an viele versteckte Orte und in dunkle Schatten führen, und er war entschlossen, ihn zu töten, wenn es an der Zeit war. Es ist der Wintermonat Dezember, der 23. Tag des Jahres 1944. Deutschland befindet sich in der Defensive, als die Alliierten beginnen, ihre einst eroberten Gebiete in immer kleinere Räume zu pressen und sie zurück in ihre ursprünglichen Länder zu treiben. Jürgen ist stolz darauf, im Alter von 17 Jahren seinen Abschluss gemacht zu haben und Mitglied der obersten deutschen Militärfraktion zu werden, die für ihre brutale Härte bekannt ist. Er war SS. Angesichts des Mangels an Männern und der Annäherung von Eindringlingen aus allen Richtungen brauchte das Oberkommando der Nazis neue Rekruten, um die Stellen der Getöteten oder Gefangenen zu füllen.

Jürgens Leidensweg begann zwei Jahre zuvor, als er seine ganze Familie in Nürnberg verlor. Er war an diesem Abend in der Kirche, spielte Musik und sang, um sich auf die Heiligabend-Aufführung am nächsten Abend vorzubereiten. Mitten in der Probe verwüsteten die alliierten Flugzeuge die Stadt.

In dieser Nacht fand er sein Haus vollständig dem Erdboden gleichgemacht und seine Familie in den Flammen verzehrt. An diesem Heiligabend traf er einen Funktionär der NSDAP, der ihm sagte: „Die Piloten und Bombenschützen waren die Juden, die entkommen sind und jetzt für die Alliierten fliegen." Jürgen verließ an diesem Tag die Kirche und machte sich auf den Weg des … Bösen.

Jürgen suchte kein Reh, kein Wildschwein oder anderes Wild … er war auf der Jagd nach Juden. Es scheint, dass es einen Ausbruch gegeben hatte und seine Befehle, alle entflohenen Juden, einschließlich Männer, Frauen und Kinder, zu finden und zu „eliminieren". Da dies sein erster Auftrag war, erwartete er die Ermordung seines ersten Juden für das, was sie ihm und seiner Familie angetan hatten. Rache und Hass waren seit dieser schicksalhaften Nacht vor zwei Jahren in das Herz des Jungen eingedrungen.

Er und seine „Jagd"-Patrouille wollten sich gerade niederlassen, als alliierte Truppen sie entdeckten und ein Kampf ausbrach. Jürgen hatte als einziger die Nacht überlebt und war in den Wald gestürmt, wo er sich den ganzen Tag versteckte, bis die Nacht wieder hereinbrach.

Es war der 24. Dezember, und dieser siebzehnjährige „Storm Trooper" war allein irgendwo im Südosten Deutschlands. Er hatte während des Gefechts seinen Kompass verloren und sein Gewehr fallen lassen;

Alles, was er hatte, war seine Luger und 6 Kugeln. Er schaffte es auch, nur ein wenig zu essen, einschließlich eines Schokoriegels, den er aufsparte.

Während er leise durch das tiefe Gestrüpp im Wald schleicht, sieht er nun in der Ferne ein schwaches Licht. Als er sich vorsichtig nähert, bemerkt er ein Häuschen neben einer ausgebombten kleinen Kirche.

Er nimmt sich Zeit, um dorthin zu gelangen, lugt leise um die Ecken und späht durch die Ritzen in den hölzernen Jalousien; einen Schatten darin zu sehen, der sich bewegt. Er nähert sich nervös der Haustür, zieht seine Pistole und tritt sie ein!

Sobald er drinnen ist, knallt er sofort die Tür hinter sich zu. Zitternd richtet er seine Luger herum und findet eine Frau vor Augen, die an einem Tisch sitzt, auf einem Regal hinter ihr viele Kerzen brennen.
Während er die Waffe auf sie gerichtet hält, sieht er sich im Raum um, um sicherzugehen, dass sie allein sind.

Jürgen sieht nun die Frau an: „Wer bist du? Wo bin ich? Welche Stadt ist das? Bist du Deutscher? „

Die Frau lächelt ruhig und steht auf, während Jürgen ihr mit seiner Pistole folgt. „Junger Mann, ich bin eine Frau und Mutter. Ich weiß, wo ich bin, und ich bin mehr als deutsch."

Verwirrt von ihren Antworten wird Jürgen etwas unruhig und beginnt auf und ab zu laufen.

Bevor er ein Wort sagen kann, spricht die Frau erneut: „Du darfst draußen im Stall bei den anderen Biestern bleiben. Geh jetzt, denn ich habe zu tun."

Jürgen denkt sich: „Wie kann diese Frau es wagen, so mit mir zu reden, ich bin SS! Ich sollte einfach ..."

Sie sieht Jürgen an und zeigt: „Geh jetzt, ich rufe dich zurück, wenn ich fertig bin."

Jürgen wird wütend ... bis er ihr in die Augen sieht und spürt, wie seine ganze Wut nachlässt. Ihr Aussehen und ihr Verhalten erinnern ihn an eine Frau, die er so liebte ... seine Mutter. Langsam öffnet er die Tür und geht hinter das Haus zu dem kleinen Stall.

Als er den kleinen Stall betritt, sieht er nur Heu zum Liegen und ein paar Wolldecken, die fein säuberlich über die Stalltüren gehängt sind. Als er nach draußen schaut, bemerkt er, dass es anfängt zu schneien. Er hätte der Frau einfach sagen sollen, sie soll in den kalten Stall gehen, das hätte ein echter SS-Soldat getan.

Als Jürgen eine warme Ecke gefunden hat, nimmt er seinen Rucksack ab, setzt sich hin und fängt an zu schauen, was er neben seinem begehrten Schokoriegel noch an Essen hat. Während er nach unten blickt, sieht er aus dem Augenwinkel eine Bewegung unter einem Heuhaufen auf der anderen Seite des Stalls.

Er springt auf, richtet seine Waffe und schreit: „Ich habe dich gesehen! Herauskommen! Komm raus oder ich schieße!"

Mit den Augen auf den Heuhaufen sieht er eine kleine Gestalt, die sich ihren Weg aus dem Heu bahnt. Langsam wird das Bild im fast dunklen Stall klar. Jürgen bemerkt eine Kerze auf einem Regal, mit einer Hand an seiner Pistole; er greift mit seinem anderen in seine Manteltasche und zieht ein Feuerzeug heraus. Beim Anzünden der Kerze entpuppt sich das Bild langsam als kleines junges Mädchen, das bis auf eine hellblaue Schleife im Haar ganz in Lumpen gekleidet ist.

Jürgen geht hinüber und stampft auf den Heuhaufen, um sich zu vergewissern, dass sie die einzige ist, die sich versteckt hat. "Wer bist du? Wie heißen Sie? Gib mir eine Antwort! Jetzt!" Jürgens Augen und Tonfall erschrecken das kleine Mädchen und sie weicht in die Ecke zurück. Jürgen schreit wieder: „Sprich zu mir! „

Als die Augen des Mädchens tränen, spricht eine leise Stimme: „Ich bin Eliana".

Jürgen sieht sie an, senkt seine Pistole, entspannt sich für eine Sekunde, packt dann das Mädchen und zieht die Ärmel ihres zerlumpten Mantels hoch, um ein Tattoo zu enthüllen. Er wirft sie zu Boden und schreit: „Jüdin!" Als er auf die kleine Gestalt herabblickte, die zurück in die Ecke kletterte, begann sich Jürgens Hass in seinen Augen zu zeigen. Schließlich waren ihre „Arten" dafür verantwortlich, dass seine ganze Familie vor zwei Jahren getötet wurde.

Er denkt sich: „Was für eine süße Rache". Er richtet seine Pistole auf das verängstigte kleine Gesicht. Jetzt ist seine Chance. Er wird seinen ersten Kill haben! Er legt langsam seinen Finger auf den Abzug und zielt auf ihren kleinen Kopf.

„Warum hasst du mich so", spricht eine kleine Stimme leise. In ihre kleinen verängstigten braunen Augen schauend, hält Jürgen für eine Sekunde inne. Zusammen mit dem glänzenden blauen Band in ihrem Haar zerreißen ihre kleinen unschuldigen Augen sein Herz.

„Das ist ein jüdischer Gedankentrick", denkt er sich. Er konzentriert sich wieder auf sie, als die Tür aufschwingt und damit Schneeflocken von draußen hereinwehen.

Bevor Jürgen die Tür schließen kann, stürmt ein kleines Lamm herein und stellt sich zwischen das Mädchen und ihn.

Jetzt sehen ihn zwei unschuldige Augenpaare an. Sein Verstand ist jetzt völlig verwirrt und er beginnt auf und ab zu gehen.

Er bleibt stehen und bellt das kleine Mädchen an: „Wo hast du das blaue Band her? „

Ohne zu zögern antwortet das junge Mädchen: „Zuerst dein Name, wenn du mich erschießen willst, zumindest dein Name."

Der von der plötzlichen Kühnheit überraschte junge Soldat antwortet: „Jürgen … jetzt du! Wo hast du es bekommen?"

„Von der netten Dame im Haus sagte sie, es sei eines meiner Geschenke. „

Jürgen ist jetzt völlig verwirrt und denkt sich, während er wie ein eingesperrtes Tier auf und ab geht: „Und jetzt? Ach, was soll ich tun? Ein Jüdin im Visier, und ein Lamm könnte ich essen"

Nach unten schauend beobachtet er den kleinen vierbeinigen, großäugigen, weißen Fellknäuel, der sich so zärtlich zwischen ihn und seine „Beute" legt.

Ein Windstoß erschüttert den Stall und ein Gegenstand fällt vom Dachsparren aufs Heu. Bei einem „Ki-ting" weiß Jürgen genau, was es ist, ein Geräusch aus glücklicheren Zeiten. Eliana und das Lamm sehen zu, wie die Luger geholstert wird und der wilde SS-Soldat ruhig hinübergeht und die Gitarre aufhebt. Wenn man es ganz leicht anschlägt, ist nur das hohe „E" verstimmt, wird aber schnell hochgestimmt.

Mit Blick auf die zwei Paar unschuldiger Augen, die ihn anstarren, sagt Jürgen ruhig: „Ich habe gespielt, seit ich zehn war. Früher habe ich in der Kirche gespielt. Ich … ich erinnere mich, wie alle kamen, um mich während der Weihnachtszeit spielen zu sehen." Auf seine kalten Fingerspitzen pusten, um sie etwas aufzuwärmen; Es dauerte nicht lange, bis Musik den schwach beleuchteten Stall erfüllte. Als Jürgen anfing, sein Lieblingslied „Stille Nacht, Heilige Nacht" zu spielen, konnte er nicht widerstehen, beim Spielen mitzusingen. Innerhalb weniger Texte begann das kleine Mädchen mitzusingen. Es war, als hätten sie geübt, vor Publikum aufzutreten. Als die beiden Stimmen den letzten Ton hielten, kehrte Ruhe in den Schutzraum ein.

Das junge Mädchen ansehend: „Du sagst, dein Name ist Eliana?" Die braunen Augen nicken nur, als ein Lächeln auf dem kostbaren kleinen Gesicht erscheint. „Eliana, wo hast du gelernt, dieses Lied zu singen?"

Mit einem noch breiteren Lächeln: „Es war die nette Dame im Haus, sie hat es für mich gesungen, nur einmal … aber irgendwie habe ich mich an alles erinnert." Etwas verwirrt blickend, spielte der Gitarrist noch ein paar Lieder, bevor er sanft das Lied legte Gitarre runter.

Jürgen saß nur da und starrte auf die beiden braunen Augenpaare, die ihn ansahen, eines mit einem Lächeln. Jürgen greift nach seinem Rucksack und holt das Erste heraus, woran seine Finger festhalten, seinen wertvollen Schokoriegel. Zu sehen, wie ein Paar Augen größer werden, überkommt etwas dieses Herz, das einst mit so viel Hass erfüllt war. Jürgen öffnet die Verpackung, bricht ein kleines Stück ab und reicht den Rest den unschuldigen Augen vor sich.

„Eliana, heute ist der 24. Dezember, ich weiß, dass die Juden das nicht feiern, aber es ist Brauch, ein Geschenk zu machen, Frohe Weihnachten."

Der einst wilde Kampfsoldat lehnt sich zurück und sieht zu, wie das kleine Mädchen jeden kleinen Bissen schätzt. Dieser Schokoriegel war sein wertvollster Besitz gewesen, aber sein größtes Vergnügen war es, ihr dabei zuzusehen, wie er ihn aß.

Nachdem sie fertig war, zeigte sie das größte Lächeln, das er je gesehen hatte: „Danke, du bist nett, nicht wie die anderen."

Eine Rührung überkam Jürgen; sein Hass war nun tot und sein Mitgefühl lebendig.

Er beginnt zu denken: „Warum? Wie war es die Schuld dieses kleinen Mädchens … das Schreckliche, was meiner Familie passiert ist? Bevor es passierte, fühlte es sich immer so gut an, Gitarre zu spielen und in der Kirche zu singen."

Ein Frieden überkam ihn, ein Gefühl, das er seit zwei Jahren nicht mehr gehabt hatte. Als Jürgen sah, dass dem kleinen Mädchen etwas kalt war, schnappte er sich eine Decke und deckte sie und das Lamm zu. Dann ging er und nahm die Gitarre und spielte, bis das Mädchen und das Lamm fest eingeschlafen waren.

Jetzt erfüllte nur noch das Geräusch zweier schnarchender Wesen den Stall, als Jürgen die Augen schloss … die erste Ruhe und Gelassenheit seit zwei Jahren.

Es fühlte sich an, als wären Stunden vergangen, als Jürgen seine Augen öffnete, um ein kleines Mädchen zu sehen, das sich zu seiner Linken kuschelte, und ein Lamm zu seiner Rechten.

Er sah auf seine Uhr, noch eine halbe Stunde bis zum Weihnachtstag. Seine Gedanken begannen, in die Vergangenheit von Weihnachten zurückzuwandern, und er konnte den Pfefferkuchen beinahe riechen und schmecken.

Als er gerade wieder die Augen schließen wollte, flüsterte eine Stimme schroff: „Jetzt musst du schnell gehen, das Böse steht vor der Tür!"

Ohne zu zögern stand der junge Soldat auf und schaute durch einen der Risse in der Stallwand. Er konnte zwei Schatten über dem mondbeschienenen offenen Feld näher kommen sehen. Er schnappte sich sein Fernglas im Taschenformat und versuchte, genauer hinzuschauen. Gerade als er fokussierte, erhellte eine Granatenexplosion in der Ferne den Himmel, seine Sicht war klar … SS!

Er denkt schnell nach, weckt Eliana mit seiner Hand vor ihrem Mund und flüstert: „Wir müssen jetzt leise gehen."

Jürgen setzt seinen Rucksack auf, wickelt Eliana in eine Decke und öffnet leise die Tür. Als die beiden fast draußen sind, beschließt ihr wütender Freund, mitzukommen.

Auf die beiden braunen Augen herablächelnd: „Du, kleines Lamm, bleib hier; es ist zu gefährlich für dich."

Damit schiebt er das Lamm mit den Füßen zurück und schließt die Tür.

Der ehemalige hasserfüllte Junge weiß, was passieren wird, wenn sie erwischt werden, er kümmert sich nicht so sehr um sich selbst, sondern um seinen neuen kleinen, unschuldigen Freund. Sie schleichen sich hinaus und versuchen, im Schatten zu bleiben. Wenn sie nur zwischen den Sträuchern bleiben können, können sie es bis in den Wald schaffen und gut versteckt sein.

Er achtet jetzt weder auf das Gewicht auf seinem Rücken noch auf seine Arme. Er bewegt sich wie eine Katze auf der Jagd. Die Sträucher enden etwa dreißig Meter vom Wald entfernt. Als die beiden schwarz gekleideten Schatten näher kommen, saust Jürgen los, als in der Ferne eine weitere Granate explodiert und ihn und Eliana enthüllt.

"Halt!!" brüllt eine Stimme. Jetzt ging es los, nur noch zehn Meter und … ein lauter Schuss, und das Bein des Jungen gab nach, und er und seine kostbare Fracht landeten im Schnee. Innerhalb von Sekunden sind die schwarzen Wölfe über ihnen. Einer leuchtet mit einer Taschenlampe auf die beiden verängstigten Seelen, die nach oben schauen.

"Du! Du bist ein SS-Soldat! Warum läufst du mit diesem kleinen Mädchen?"

Der andere Mann geht hinüber und zieht instinktiv Elianas Ärmel hoch, während das Licht das Geheimnis preisgibt.
„Jüdin! Du versuchst, diesen kleinen Jüdin zu retten?"

Ohne zu zögern bellt eine tapfere Jungenstimme im gleichen Ton zurück: „Ja! Sie ist meine Freundin!"

Die beiden SS-Männer starren die beiden am Boden an, dann einander an und fangen an zu lachen. Einer schultert sein Gewehr und zückt seine Luger. Jürgen beginnt im Schnee nach seinem zu tasten, aber ohne Erfolg.

Mit einem breiten Grinsen im Gesicht lacht das Biest mit der Luger, dann räuspert es sich: „Dummer Junge, du hast unseren Kodex verraten, dafür bist du zum Tode verurteilt. Aber nicht, bis du diesen dreckigen kleinen Jüdin vor dir sterben siehst!"

Er spannt die Pistole, zielt auf Eliana und schießt, aber nicht bevor Jürgen ihren kleinen Körper mit seinem abschirmt. Als die Kugel in seinen Körper eindringt, entbrennt er vor Schmerz.

Der andere SS-Mann zieht seine Pistole: „Blöder Junge, na kleiner Jüdin, ihr beide werdet den Aasfressern zum Fraß werden!"

Als er seine Pistole spannt, hallen zwei laute Schüsse durch die Nacht, und jetzt liegen zwei Leichen im Schnee und färben ihn mit einem dampfenden roten Strom.

Nun sind Schritte zu hören, die sich eilig den beiden Leichen nähern.

Eine Stimme durchbricht die Stille: „Hey Mac! Tolles Schießen! …. Du hast diese beiden Schweinehunde, sie sind toter als tot!"

Eliana sieht zu, wie weitere Männer in grünen Uniformen sie umringen. Zu Jürgen kriechend und umarmend sagt sie leise: „Er ist mein Freund"

Einer der GI ruft: „Hey Karl … komm her. Ich glaube, dieses kleine Mädchen versucht uns etwas auf Kraut zu sagen." Der Mann kommt vorbei und Eliana erzählt ihm von Jürgen und wie er nett ist und sie gerettet hat.

Ein Mann mit einem roten Kreuz auf dem Helm kommt herüber und wirft einen Blick auf den verwundeten Jungen vor sich. "Armer Junge, er hat nicht viel Zeit, sieht aus wie eine Leberspritze."

Karl übersetzt dies Eliana, während Tränen ihre Augen füllen. Jürgen blickt auf und lächelt Eliana an: „Weine nicht um mich, du bist sicher und ich werde bald bei meiner Familie sein."

Eliana nimmt die blaue Schleife ab, die ihr die Dame geschenkt hat, und bindet sie um Jürgens Hals. „Frohe Weihnachten, mein Freund" Eliana sagt dem Übersetzer jetzt, dass es ein Haus mit nur einer Dame gibt, ganz in der Nähe, und könnten sie bitte ihre Freundin dorthin bringen, aus dem Schnee.

Als Tränen ihre Augen füllen, tragen ein paar rotäugige GIs die lebensgefährlich verletzte Retterin zum Haus.

Der GI klopft, als die Dame die Tür öffnet, „Sprichst du Deutsch?" fragt Karl.

Die Dame lächelt und antwortet auf Englisch: „Ich spreche viele Sprachen".

Die GI's tragen Jürgen hinein und erzählen der Dame von seinem Schicksal. Eliana legt ihn auf eine Pritsche und umarmt ihren Helden erneut.

Jürgen kann nicht umhin, zufrieden mit seinem Handeln zu sein.

Ein plötzlicher Knall in der Ferne und ein Mann schreit: „Schnapp dir das Mädchen, los geht's!"

Tränen fallen aus diesen kleinen braunen Augen auf ihren Freund und er flüstert: „Geh jetzt und bleib in Sicherheit. Erinnere dich an mich, wenn du alt und grau bist … ich liebe dich".

Das kleine Mädchen wird fortgetragen, und die Augen des Jungen schließen sich der Dunkelheit.

Die Dame kniet vor ihm und sieht zu, wie die GIs gehen. „Geh, ich werde mich darum kümmern, ich und mein Sohn im Stall."

Wie Sand in einer Sanduhr waren die Jahre im Handumdrehen vergangen. Eliana war zur Hochzeit ihrer Enkelin nach Deutschland zurückgekehrt. Siebzig Jahre sind vergangen. Es war wieder einmal Heiligabend, als Eliana und ihre Familie durch die deutsche Landschaft fuhren. Als sie an einer kleinen Stadt vorbeikam, fiel ihr ein Gebäude ins Auge: „Halt! Wir müssen aufhören!"

Ihre Enkelinnen, die bald GI-Ehemänner werden, hielten das Auto an, weil sie dachten, dass etwas nicht stimmte.

Eliana deutete: „Da. Fahr mich dorthin."

Als sie anhielten, stieg Eliana aus dem Auto und ging zur Vorderseite des Gebäudes … machte sich bereit, hineinzugehen. „Oma, was machst du da? Das ist eine Kirche, keine Synagoge."

Sie winkt allen zu, tritt ein und setzt sich. Als sie sich umschaut, lächelt sie: „Ich kenne diesen Ort, er hat nicht so ausgesehen, aber das kleine Haus nebenan ist fast immer noch dasselbe."

Als sie die verwirrten Gesichter ihrer Familie sah, „Ich habe vor langer, langer Zeit einer Freundin ein Versprechen gegeben, das ich nicht vergessen habe …"

Ein Priester kommt heraus und fragt auf Deutsch, ob er ihnen helfen könne. Er erklärt, dass die Heiligabendmesse erst später in der Nacht stattfinden würde und sie sich darauf vorbereiten, dafür zu proben. Eliana erklärt, dass sie aus Amerika stammt, aber als kleines Mädchen einmal hier war und sich gerade an eine Freundin erinnerte, die damals hier starb.

In Elianas braune Augen schauend, voller Kummer, lächelt der Priester und schüttelt den Kopf „Ja".

Wie Eliana sich an jene Nacht vor so langer Zeit erinnert, wird in der vorderen Ecke der Kirche eine Gitarre gestimmt.

Es beginnt bald ein bekanntes Lied zu spielen, das sie in dieser Nacht zum ersten Mal im Stall hörte und seitdem jedes Jahr hört. Zuhause in Amerika heißt es Stille Nacht.

Eliana singt zum Erstaunen ihrer Familie leise mit. Als sie fertig ist, sagt sie mit einer Träne im Auge ihrer Familie, dass sie dem Gitarristen danken muss.

Sie winkt dem Priester zu, der sie bleiben ließ, und flüstert ihm zu: „Kann ich hochgehen und dem Gitarristen danken? Das war so schön, und obwohl ich Jüdin bin, berührt dieses Lied mein altes Herz."

"Na sicher! Das ist das Beste, was ich von Pater Johann dieses Lied gehört habe."

Eliana sagt ihrer Familie, dass sie gleich wieder da ist und geht nach vorne, rutscht hinter Pater Johann hinein, klopft ihm auf die Schulter und flüstert: „Vielen Dank, Sie haben das Leben einer alten Dame komplett gemacht. Ich bin Jude, aber ein netter Junge hat mir das einmal vorgespielt und mich in dieser Nacht vor siebzig Jahren auch gerettet."

Pater Johann legt seine Gitarre hin und sagt: „Sie sagte, ich würde dich wiedersehen, bevor ich sterbe. Ich habe nie aufgehört zu glauben."

Als er langsam aufsteht und sich umdreht, war Eliana verblüfft zu sehen, dass es ein alter Priester war, der dieses Lied gespielt hatte. Als sie genauer hinsah, konnte sie Tränen in seinen Augen sehen. Dann sah sie um seinen weißen Kragen herum etwas, das ihre Augen ebenfalls zum Fließen brachte.

Ein verblasstes blaues Band.

„Eliana! Eliana!" Die beiden umarmen sich nun zum Erstaunen aller in der Kirche.

„Jürgen … wie? Du bist gestorben, ich erinnere mich"

Beide setzen sich Arm in Arm, während der jetzige Pater Johann die Geschichte erzählt, „Ich erinnere mich, dass du … Dunkelheit … dann Licht verlassen hast. Dann waren die Dame und das Lamm neben mir. Da hörte ich sie sagen: „Lieber Junge, mach dir keine Sorgen, du wirst sie wiedersehen, bevor du stirbst". Als ich aufwachte, waren dieselben Soldaten zurück und brachten mich in ein Krankenhaus. Sie nannten mich ein Weihnachtswunder."

Eliana noch immer geschockt: „Und was ist aus der Lady geworden? Hast du sie wiedergesehen?«

Jürgen steht auf und nimmt Eliana an die Hand: „Komm, ich will dir was zeigen."

Jetzt von ihrer Familie gefolgt, bleibt Jürgen stehen und zeigt: „Da … als ich diese Kirche wieder aufgebaut habe, habe ich sie gefunden."

Alle sind wie gebannt, denn an der Wand hängt ein Bild der Dame von vor so langer Zeit. Unter dem Gemälde von ihr mit einem blauen Band im Haar befindet sich eine Plakette mit der Aufschrift:

„Die Jungfrau Maria"

More tales by B. Diamond, available NOW!

Tales of Christmas Volume 1

Tales of Terror Volume 1

DiamondDiAngeloPublishing@yahoo.com

2022 Diamond-DiAngelo Music and Books

We Wish You a Very Merry Christmas, this Year, and for Many Years to Come!

Thank You for Sharing Christmas with Us ...

H. P. Golding and R. H. Bauderer

Bobby Diamond and Rodney DiAngelo

Silent Night,

Holy Night

Made in the USA
Middletown, DE
08 November 2022